IF YOU DARE

JESSICA LEMMON

Previously released on Entangled's Flaunt imprint – November 2013 and has been enhanced with new material.

Entangled Publishing, LLC
2614 South Timberline Road
Suite 109
Fort Collins, CO 80525
Visit our website at www.entangledpublishing.com.

Lovestruck is an imprint of Entangled Publishing, LLC.

Edited by Liz Pelletier
Cover design by Heather Howland
Cover art from iStock

Manufactured in the United States of America

Second Edition July 2015

For Niki
The sister I never had, but got to choose.

Chapter One

Stupid, stupid, stupid.

Lily McIntire pulled to a stop in the crumbling driveway of 102 Willow Street in Fantom, Ohio. Dust settled around her car, revealing the decaying building in front of her, its slats weather-beaten, front door padlocked, and porch stairs splintering. You know, the place where she'd be getting absolutely *no* sleep tonight.

She chewed on her lip and reconsidered leaving the sanctuary of her car. But she had to. A gauntlet had been thrown, and thrown by a man she refused to lose to. Again.

Dammit.

"Probably just full of spiders, anyway," she said aloud as she unbuckled her seat belt. Her voice came out paper-thin and *not* infused with the courage she so desperately needed, but she ignored that. She also ignored the fact that she hated spiders, and any number of creepy-crawly things, all of which were probably living in communal harmony inside the decrepit building. "Look at the bright side," she grumbled, climbing out of the car. "Spiders are better than what is allegedly lurking around here."

This might have been the one and only case where spiders were preferable.

It seemed dangerous to admit even to herself that she was scared half out of her wits just being there, let alone *staying overnight*. But she sure as hell wasn't going to give Marcus Black the satisfaction of winning the stupidest bet on earth.

One night in Willow Mansion would get her a four-day, five-night trip to Hawaii. All expenses included. And after two years of busting her hump as one of two lead designers at Cameron Designs, she had earned it. The dare Marcus threw at her feet? It was a no brainer. And if she lost, she'd owe him one date. One *work* date. She could do this. She *would* do this.

Straightening her shoulders, she tromped to the front of the house, kicking loose gravel and crunching a stray leaf here and there. The foliage had changed from green to burnished gold a few weeks ago. Some leaves still stubbornly clung to the trees, but the majority lay strewn in the overgrown grass and clogging the warped gutters overhead.

Lovely.

Other than a few obvious building code violations, the house didn't appear *too* oppressive in the streaming sunlight. And under the wide, bowing maples, dappled with late September sunshine, Willow Mansion was almost...well... *charming*. Not that she'd recommend refurbishing it into a summer home or anything, but one night wouldn't be that bad. A pleasant breeze kicked Lily's hair and stuck a few stray strawberry-blond tendrils to her lip gloss. She tugged them away and smiled at the relic before her with newfound appreciation. Maybe all the rumors about the mansion had been wildly exaggerated.

A creak sounded overhead, and she diverted her attention to the upstairs windows. An ancient shutter shifted on its hinges, let out a grating whine, and fell from its precarious perch. She leaped to the right, a pathetic squeak trembling in her throat as the shutter crashed to the ground and sent a spray of pebbles onto her shoes. Heart hammering against her ribs, she glanced upward again and reconsidered going inside. Spiders or ghosts were now the least of her worries. Having a ceiling collapse in on her, on the other hand…

"Get me through this," she said to the Man Upstairs through clenched teeth. "And I'll never drink tequila again."

Yes. Tequila. All bad ideas started with tequila. And usually ended with them, too.

After work on Wednesday, she'd allowed herself to be talked into a celebratory shot-and-beer night by her (mostly) well-meaning coworkers. They'd just won the bid on Reginald London Superstores. The first would open in Ohio in June of next year, and their winning interior design drawing had been chosen over at least twelve other big-name firms. London was a huge coup for Cameron Designs, and the account would bring in more profit than Lily's best friend, Joanie Cameron, had seen since she and her husband, Clive, launched their firm a little over two years ago. Lily was beyond proud of her friends, who deserved every good thing that came their way. It had taken them nearly three months of late nights and working on weekends to complete the proposal, but their team prevailed as the little-foursome-that-could.

Then there was the matter of her co-designer, asshat Marcus Black…

Though a consummate prankster, the man was an integral part—if not the superior cog—of knocking this one out of the park, but it didn't mean she had to swoon over him like the rest of the female population. Just thinking of him raised her hackles—his know-it-all attitude, his cocky, better-than-you half smile, the train of blondes he paraded at the annual Retail Space Design dinner every year. This year, he would be accepting the coveted Designer of the Year award. If the award were judged on personality, she was sure he'd have lost to someone far more pedigreed.

And now she was being mean. She couldn't help it. She'd been vying for that award since the start of her career four and a half years ago and was sure (sure!) that this year she'd nailed it. Add that to the fact she'd lost a recent tit for tat contest with the man, and she had more than a few wounds to lick.

So, Marcus wasn't quite the asshat she'd like to continue convincing herself he was, and honestly, there were times when his half smile stirred parts of her below the skirt better left unmentioned. And that know-it-all attitude and string of sharp-barbed jokes often came with a good-natured grin, punctuated by a deep dimple in one cheek.

Her heart fluttered as she thought of him now, and she immediately chastised herself. Attractive or not, dating her co-worker was strictly off-limits. Forever. If she ever expected to be respected—to win the RSD Designer of the Year award for herself—she couldn't think with her girl-parts. She was more brains than boobs, no matter what her ex thought of her.

Still, she'd let her imagination cross a line on occasion. Like on one particularly late night, when she and Marcus were hovering over several designs and a few containers of Kung Pao chicken. She'd watched in awe as he slid his pencil over a fresh sheet of paper, sketching the design that would be the one London preferred better than all of the others. Retail space layout wasn't the sexiest of interior architecture, but Marcus wore it well. His capability spoke for itself, and watching that undeniably masculine hand dusted in dark hair move across the paper was like watching a painter capture a sunset with amazing accuracy. She'd leaned over him, captivated, while his aftershave tingled her senses, and his deep voice penetrated her shell. The rare moment of amicable peace between them made her wonder if she'd misjudged him initially.

"Whatever."

She *needed* to believe that Marcus, with his serial dating history and captivating brand of charm, was no different than the other talented, good-looking jerks she'd dated in the past. Then she could avoid him. If she could only get her hormones on board with her very astute mind, then she'd have no problem preventing a situation like the last one she escaped.

At the thought of Emmett, her lip curled. No. She wasn't willing to repeat the mistakes she'd made with a certain degenerate man-whore in the past. Marcus may not be as classless as Emmett, but it didn't stop her mantra of *"Never again"* from dancing through her head.

At the thought, her heels dug in deeper, and she made a wide arc around the downed shutter and opened her trunk.

Crowbar in hand, she approached the door, testing the tool's weight. She'd never broken into a building before. The only lock-breaking experience she had was when she'd busted the little silver one on her older sister's diary. Admittedly...not the same. She took one last glance around the grounds to ensure she was alone, shoved the crowbar into the rusted *U* of the padlock, and gave it a sharp pull. The lock popped open and thudded onto the warped wooden porch.

"Ha!" An unexpected sense of accomplishment surged through her. "See?" She bent to retrieve the lock, tossed it into the air, and caught it in her palm. "I'm not uptight."

Which was exactly what she'd been trying to prove to Marcus on Wednesday night when she went to the bar to celebrate the contract. He thought she had a stick up her ass, and she'd intended on proving him wrong. While she often went home to a frozen pizza, he was the one dating half the town. Maybe three-quarters. Hard to say. So, two days ago, Lily let his harmless jabs at her power suit roll off her back, had gracefully accepted his challenge to a game of pool, and even proved she could hang out in a dive bar by shedding her fitted blazer and tossing it over a torn leather stool.

When she'd first come to Cameron Designs after leaving her former job, Marcus had caught her eye. No denying the way his stubble perfectly rimmed his lips, or the tumble of dark hair begging her fingers *touch me*. On another plane, she could have easily fallen for his charm. He'd asked her out, after all. She'd been there a few short weeks and he sidled into her office and leaned on her desk and asked her out for dinner. Not drinks. Not coffee. "This new Italian place," he'd said. The part of her that would have said yes *before* Emmett was gone, and had apparently absconded with her manners but not her sanity. She'd replied with a curt, "No." Marcus took the rejection with surprising grace, but then the jabs started. Like a kid in school pulling her pigtails, he hadn't let up since.

She would have been flattered if she wasn't so determined to never date anyone ever again in the history of time and space. But then afterward, they'd settled into a comfortable rivalry. Marcus teased her at work, and joked profusely, and she ignored the fact he dated like it was a sport. Honestly, she figured he had asked her out because he asked *everyone* out. He was a dating machine. She...wasn't. Her bandaged reputation couldn't afford to be.

So in comparison, she was definitely the more rigid of the two of them. Somehow on Wednesday night, after two tequila shots followed by two or three bottles of beer—she couldn't remember—his jabs turned into charm and she had not only been baited into this lamebrain bet, she'd *insisted* on it.

"I'm not as girlie as you think, you know," she'd said, one hand wrapped around her pool stick, the other propped primly on her hip.

Marcus, who had been racking the pool balls at the other end of the table, paused to grunt at her statement before moving the eight ball to the center position and rolling the triangle into place.

That smug sound never failed to raise her ire. Chapping her ass seemed to be a talent Marcus Black had mastered. And she didn't want him to think less of her. She wasn't really sure *what* she wanted from him, but she did want to impress him. He impressed her all the time without even trying.

Like right then, when he lifted the triangle off the balls and not one of them wiggled out of its spot.

She searched for the memory of one thing she'd done in her life that might make her seem less of a fuddy-duddy. The moment she thought of one, she flashed him a smile. "When I was in the eighth grade, my friend Valerie and I hiked up to Willow Mansion."

Long believed to be a local haunt, the mansion was a hotbed of paranormal rumors and teenaged debauchery. Everyone in Fantom knew of the story behind the mansion, the likely overblown tale of the woman who fell to her death from a second story window. Maybe it was true, maybe it wasn't. But everyone thought it was, so she figured she'd use that as her badge of bravery. Proof she could hang with the tough kids.

Instead, Marcus spared her a dry glance, his hooded eyes wholly unimpressed.

Figured.

"On Halloween," she lied, amping up her street cred. "Night." The more she added, the lamer she sounded. She shut up while she was ahead.

Removing the triangle from the carefully arranged balls, he flipped it end over end in a smooth, annoyingly graceful motion. She bet he never fumbled anything. Meanwhile, she was sporting a coffee stain on her skirt from a mishap at Tim Horton's that morning. Like she had in the past, she took a moment to admire his strong hands—capable of precision and artistry, but manly and rough enough to make her wonder what they'd feel like on the soft skin at the back of her neck. A fantasy that could have been reality if she'd said yes to Italian that day long ago. But it was too late to go back now. If he ever meant it at all.

She blinked out of her little alcohol-induced fantasy, a daydream that was not entirely her fault. The man really was too attractive for his own good—that natural bad boy swagger, the defined sinew of his forearms, and his voice, low and gravelly with a hint of humor, as showcased when he spoke next.

"Yeah, right. You wouldn't last an hour in that place." He raised one dark eyebrow and added, "What did you do, run up, touch the front door, then run giggling down the driveway?"

She gave him an exaggerated eye roll and hoped it was convincing. The scene he'd described was *exactly* what her friend Val had done. Lily hadn't been as brave. A good fifty feet away from the house, her fair skin baking under the bright noonday sun, she'd shouted at Valerie to hurry up before they got caught.

Okay, so maybe she was the rigid good girl. But she'd tried to break the rules once—dating her ex had been against workplace policy—and she'd paid dearly. Following rules was smart. She was one of the best designers of retail spaces large and small. She had guts. She had moxie. She had…freckles. And she felt each one of those scattered dots vanish under her blush of embarrassment at Marcus's insight.

Of course he noticed. He came closer, his pool cue in one hand. "I knew it." He tapped her nose with his forefinger, his voice low and sensual. Parts of her leaned closer to him. The parts that shouldn't.

She straightened purposefully. "I'll bet you I could." Her voice was smaller than she would've liked, but she forced herself to meet his eyes. Sort of. He grinned and her gaze trickled down to the dimple indenting his left cheek. She stared at it a beat too long, wondering idly how a man with whitened teeth and supple lips could still look rugged and manly.

"All night?" That close to her, his innuendo-loaded, two-word question sent her blood pumping extra fast through her veins and made her briefly entertain a mini-fantasy about what he would be like in bed. It'd been a while since she'd been in bed with anyone other than her vibrator, so what did she know? So, she imagined. Just for fun. Just for a second. She wouldn't be the least bit surprised to find he took his time exploring her body. Or if he laid his tongue on her skin and drew long, slow lines down her limbs just like he did when he set pencil to paper. She'd noticed that when he'd sketched the design for London's retail store. The way Marcus almost... *savored* each and every line. The careful way he cradled the lead, the smooth motion of his hand sliding over the paper. The scraping sound as each line formed before her eyes... The way she imagined his stubble would scrape on her neck.

On her bare breasts...

"Your break," he said.

She snapped her shoulders back.

"You didn't answer me."

It was a full five seconds before she recalled what they'd been talking about. Her imagination was snagged between the brambles of the fantasy of his mouth, and the idea that she could use that as fodder for her date with her vibrator. Dragging her eyes from his face, she chalked the end of her cue stick with way, *way* too much concentration. "Yes. All night."

"You're on." He slid around behind her, his body heat enveloping her, his warm breath fanning her hair and causing her nape to tingle.

Turned on, maybe.

"Hundred bucks."

She moved away from him, palming her throat to catch her breath. The scratch of his voice, his very presence, threw her majorly off-kilter. She had to regain her focus, get her feet under her again. With a new sense of purpose, she leaned over the racked balls.

Infusing her own voice with confidence, she said, "Come on, Marcus. We just made *thousands* of bucks from our bonuses on the London account. I think a bet like this one calls for higher stakes." She cracked the cue ball into the center of the arranged balls. Lame. Her shot did little more than roll the colorful orbs a few inches from their original resting places.

Behind her again, he grasped her hips with wide, warm hands—she assumed to move her to the side. But before he did, he squeezed his fingers into her skirt, just enough to dance along the line of "inappropriate". Only it didn't feel inappropriate. She felt like backing her ass into his crotch. Pressing her head into his chest. Maybe rubbing against him a little… Right when she might have done just that, he moved to her left, robbing her of his heat and attention, and positioned himself over the cue ball.

A fine sheen of sweat lingered on her brow and she reached for her drink, unsure if the beer would help or hinder her at this point, and not caring either way.

"Fine." He paused over the table and shot her a look

laced with dark promises. "A thousand."

She cleared her throat and adjusted her skirt as if she could wipe away the twin heated imprints of his hands on her body, or the look in his eyes that made her wonder for a split second if she might *not* regret sleeping with him. Even if it only lasted one night. Then she remembered her last workplace tragedy and decided that sex with a coworker was *so* the worst idea. He leaned over the table, and she appreciated the way his jeans outlined his perfect butt, and the way the snug cotton T-shirt molded over one muscular shoulder as he drew back the pool cue. She couldn't help it. And she figured as a female it was her duty to notice a specimen this delicious. So long as she kept her clothes on when he was around, no harm, no foul.

Proving his body was for more than just admiring, his shot smacked into the balls and scattered them across the table with a satisfying *crack!* A solid sank into one corner and another dipped into the side pocket.

But of course.

"You have big ones." A smile tilted his lips on his stubbled face.

"Excuse me?"

"Stripes," he said. "They look bigger than the solids."

"Oh." She shook her head, pretending frustration, but mainly it was to get her brain back online. *Note to self: Tequila makes you attracted to unworthy men.*

They'd been discussing something before she'd lost time ogling him…oh, right. The bet. If not money, what? Then she landed on it, digging an idea out of the part of her brain not marinating in Jose Cuervo. "Hawaii."

His aim slipped, sending the white ball into the corner

pocket. He straightened, his smile vanishing as if dry-erased from his face. "I won that trip fair and square."

"That's debatable."

Joanie and Clive had intended the trip as a second honeymoon, until Clive learned he'd be at a work-related conference during the first weekend in December. The Camerons put their trip on the line as a reward to the designer who could win the most accounts in two months. Lily and Marcus were neck and neck the entire contest…until Marcus had won by one account.

"You submitted your drawings to Alan the same day I did," he said, petulant.

Alan. His cousin. Like she would have had a prayer of winning the bid to redesign the svelte coffee shop's interior! True, a win was a win for Cameron Designs, and normally they were all on the same team. But her competitive nature had flamed hot during that contest. Losing to Marcus stung.

She wanted Hawaii. Hell, she wanted to *win*.

On my own. With no one's help. Yeah, that. Emmett, her ex-boyfriend's stupid face popped into her mind again. Why was she thinking of him so much lately? Maybe because this was the first time she'd really felt like her spark was back. Marcus had fed that flicker, and now she was alight.

She crossed her arms and refocused on her goal. How to get a do-over from Marcus? "What's the matter?" she teased, baiting him. "Too scared to put Hawaii on the line?"

Her suggestion shouldn't have worked. It was immature and childish… But his jaw ticked in challenge, and she found herself tamping down the smile dying to produce itself on her face. Simply say the word "scared" to the man and he'd break his neck trying to prove he wasn't.

"You'd have to stay the entire night," he finally said.

Ha! She had him. "Done."

"Alone."

"Done."

"This Friday. The thirteenth."

"D-Done."

Chapter Two

Halfway back to her car, her phone buzzed from the pocket of her jeans. She knew who it was without looking. Sure enough, a text message from Mr. Wonderful read, THERE YET FRAIDY CAT?

Ignore him, a mature, self-reliant voice asserted.

After debating for two seconds, she keyed in the word JERKWAD and sent the text.

She'd never been good at listening to reason. *Obviously.* She angled her head up to the second story, where filthy windows clouded with dust and decay seemed to transform into yawning faces with soulless eyes. The human brain often put together random shapes into an order it could understand, she knew. There were no faces gaping back at her from the upstairs window, just her overactive imagination seeing things where it shouldn't.

She closed her eyes and then reopened them. Nothing but dirty glass and yellowed lace curtains. A shudder snaked up her spine anyway.

She spun on the heel of one sneaker, went to her trunk again, and dragged out a giant tote filled with bedding, a shiny new Coleman lantern, and a few hundred dollars' worth of supplies from the local sporting goods store. Then she hauled her booty up the short staircase to the door and kicked it open.

Marcus would laugh his tight butt off if he saw her lugging all this crap in to stay one night. But "roughing it" wasn't part of the bet.

They had finished their beers and game shortly after the dare was made. Marcus had won, further fueling her flair for competition.

"When you succumb to white hot terror and run screaming into the hills"—he'd tugged his brown bomber jacket over impossibly wide shoulders, and she'd tried really, really hard not to admire the way the chest muscles rippled with the movement—"what do I get?"

"What, my terror and abject humiliation aren't enough?"

"Satisfying, but no."

She'd pressed her lips together to keep from smiling and asked, "What did you have in mind?"

He hadn't hesitated. "The annual RSD dinner."

"That's it? I go to that every year."

"As my date," he'd clarified.

She doubted she'd successfully hidden her shock. The man had shown up to the last three Retail Space Design dinners with a different blonde du jour. It wasn't as if he was hard up for a woman to accompany him. His dates' duties seemed to include: laughing at his jokes, holding champagne flutes between perfectly manicured fingers, and worshipping his every footstep.

She pictured herself in that role and snorted.

He sent a long, slow gaze up and down her body and she swore she felt it like a sizzling brand. "Do you own any outfits that *don't* make you look like you never miss a *Wall Street Journal*?"

Self-consciously, she fingered the two buttons holding her Calvin Klein blazer closed. "I like this suit."

He took a deliberate step closer, making her face grow warm. "I didn't say I didn't like the suit." His suggestive murmur, and the way he brushed her fingers aside to touch a button on her jacket drew her in. She found herself staring at his mouth, evaluating the shape of his lips, and calculating how far she'd have to rise on her toes to press her lips to his. *Not far.*

She came to her senses, albeit a bit late, but managed to jerk away from him. He backed off instantly, his eyes shuttering, his smug grin locking back into place. Did she imagine the moment of mutual lust?

"When I win," he said, "You have to wear a cocktail dress."

"I do own a cocktail dress, you know."

"A short one."

"It's short. I have great legs." She noticed his eyes slide down her body again and she resisted the urge to squirm.

"And no panties."

"Marcus!" She crossed her arms defiantly, but felt her face go hot at the suggestion. Felt *all* of her go hot at the suggestion.

"It's Hawaii," he said, spreading his arms wide. "If you expect me to toss it into this bet, you need to up the ante on your side." She tried to laugh him off, but he stared her down while she waited for her cab. Finally, when the yellow-checkered vehicle pulled up, he prompted her with, "We agree, then?"

On the way home, she would try and figure out why he would ask her to be his date to the dinner he likely already *had* a date for. He had to be messing with her. She'd shot down his advances before. Maybe this was him taunting her, trying to put the one thing on the line that would make her balk. If he thought she would let Hawaii go on the prospect of her going sans-underpants, he had another thing coming.

"No panties," she shot back, noting the helpful cabbie had stepped out of the car and craned an interested eyebrow. "But you can't touch me below the shoulders."

The slow spread of his smile made her tingle everywhere. "Oh, honey. You have no idea what I'm capable of above the shoulders."

It was the thought that had followed her all the way home. And into bed.

Of course, the next morning she plodded into work with the mother of all hangovers. Not to miss a chance to tip the scales, Marcus made sure to try and psyche her out as often as possible.

He swung into her office, holding onto the doorframe with one hand and gripping a crowbar in the other. "Hope the cops don't catch you. B and Es include fines and jail time." If she'd been a hundred percent, she would have Googled his claim to see if it were true. Instead, she'd held out a hand and accepted the length of iron.

This morning, she was sipping her second cup of coffee when the email icon at the bottom of her computer screen flickered.

Lil, thought you might like to know who you're up against tonight. Happy Friday the 13th! M.

She opened the attachment, and then wished she hadn't. A scanned newspaper article, so old the edges of the periodical were torn and faded, boasted the header: **WOMAN FALLS TO HER DEATH, POLICE SAY SUICIDE.** Lily read through the article about Essie Mae Epson and her leap from the second story window. The article was tame compared to the rich urban legend that surrounded the place. The rumors of Essie's suicide being a murder at her husband's hands, the phantom voices on the property, a woman in white, and the general feeling of unease...

But that's all they are. Rumors.

Now, standing outside of Willow Mansion, the world seemed utterly normal.

The birds chirped, the leaves rustled in the breeze, and cars and semis rumbled down the highway in the distance. Friday the thirteenth or not, she was standing in warm sunlight, breathing air infused with the fragrances of fall, and the big, scary mansion appeared more neglected than eerie.

Yes, the "Legend of Essie Mae" still looped her brain like a stock car in a race, but she found herself wondering if a woman named Essie had ever actually lived there. She had no proof the article about Essie's suicide wasn't Photoshopped. Marcus was a designer, and she wouldn't put it past him to stack the deck in his favor. He was a practical joker at his core.

Besides, she *had* this. She may have balked at age fourteen, but now an adult, she could look at the house as just a structure. A structure that was an eyesore, not the site of a demonic possession. But the thought supposed to make her feel better somewhat stalled her mental rounds of "For She's a Jolly Good Fellow."

Keeping her toes lined up with the threshold, she poked just her chin into the house. Boarded-up windows lined the other side of the murky living room, dust motes kicking up in the streams of sunlight eking their way through the gaps of the boards. To the right stood what appeared to be a treacherous staircase. The steps were warped, the railing missing every other spindle. With one final steadying breath, she hoisted her supplies in her arms, steeled her spine, and stepped inside.

The pungent aroma of waterlogged floorboards hit her first. The light poking through showed no more than the gloomy outline of a leaf-strewn floor and a decaying stone fireplace.

Okay, so at the moment, she didn't feel like she *had this*. What she felt mostly…was creeped out.

Something skittered up the patterned wallpaper to her right, but she refused to turn her head. Her peripheral vision made out enough of the long, shining body and waving antennae to know who she'd be bunking with tonight. She shuddered.

Unfortunately, she hadn't thought to put Raid on her shopping list.

Disgust sat like a lump in her throat, but she gulped it down with purpose and tossed her supplies onto the center of the living room floor. The massive space would make for a workable ground zero. She could blow up the air mattress and surround herself with the comforts of home. It probably wouldn't even feel like an allegedly haunted mansion by the time she got set up.

She kicked a downed spindle, and it rolled and hit the baseboard at the edge of the staircase with an echoing *thud*. One last thought about the shadow-faces peering down at her from upstairs, and it was decided: downstairs would have to do. No way was she going anywhere near the second story.

A doorway stood to her left, and she ventured over, poking her head inside. The wide kitchen was big enough for several servants, and well lit thanks to a few large, still-intact windows on that side of the house. But the warped linoleum, bones of dead mice or rats—hard to say at that level of decomposition—and door-less cabinets encrusted with cobwebs kept the room from being mistaken for cozy.

Funny, she thought as she turned back, *the living room is charming by comparison.*

A loud *bang* made her jump and a pathetic little *Meep!* exit her lips. The front door hung open, leaves blowing across the entryway. After her heart restarted, she blew out a breath of relief. It was only the wind. Likely a sister gust to the one that had dropped that shutter so near her head earlier.

Certainly not a ghost trying to spook her out of her room and board for the night.

A few structural uncertainties weren't going to send her fleeing. Wouldn't Marcus love that? If one little bump in the waning daylight sent her running…Nuh-uh. No way. He wasn't winning this bet before it started.

If the only prize from this ridiculous bet was her proving she was strong and brave and capable, then it would be worth it. Even better, she could reflect on her personal growth while sipping a rum-infused drink out of a hulled coconut in Oahu. Ah, that made her smile.

She made one final trip outside to retrieve the rest of her supplies. As she shouldered her purse, she recalled Marcus's smug expression as she'd pulled that same handbag over her shoulder at the bar on Wednesday. He thought she was girlie and delicate, but she was about to prove herself part warrior. Or something.

Let's do this.

Bravery renewed, she reminded herself she'd suffer nothing worse than dust allergies during her night behind the mansion's walls.

The grocery bag in the crook of her arm was filled with the essentials. Wine, *check*. Bottled water, *check*. iPad, *check*. Dinner from her favorite local restaurant, *check*.

At the mansion's front door, she cast one last look at the surrounding woods and long, cracked driveway. She'd parked off to one side, behind a low-hanging weeping willow and overgrown brush. Satisfied her car was hidden from the road, she punched the lock button on her key fob and smiled at the answering cheery beep.

"Hawaii, here I come." With that last thought warming her, she headed into the dark house and shut the door behind her.

Chapter Three

"I don't know why I had to come with you."

Marcus stopped climbing the weed-infested hill to glare at his recently-turned-wussy best friend. "What are you bitching about? I'm the one with Hawaii on the line."

"Yeah, and that trip was technically mine." Clive pointed the flashlight into Marcus's face. "Plus, I'm the one in danger of an early grave if Joanie finds out we aren't really playing darts at the Shot Spot."

Marcus shielded his eyes, and Clive swept the beam off his face. "I swear you traded in your balls at the altar a year and a half ago."

His buddy only smiled. "That's a helluva trade, considering how much sex I get."

"Married people don't have sex," Marcus grumbled, resuming his climb to Willow Mansion. "Everyone knows that."

"Yes we do. But unlike you, I don't have to sneak out in

my underwear in the morning."

Rather than argue, mainly because Clive had made a compelling and, other than the underwear part, an irritatingly accurate point, Marcus continued his stealthy approach to the mansion. As stealthy as one could be toting a duffel bag full of Halloween costumes.

Hey. It was *Hawaii*. He may as well try to salvage it.

They rounded the house and found a reasonably clean window that hadn't been busted out. Marcus peeked through one lower corner and Clive through the other. He could make out a kitchen, and beyond that, a doorway. Lily's face was lit with ambient light one room over.

Marcus swore under his breath. "Is that…sushi?"

Clive chuckled.

His strawberry-blond, lethally sexy co-worker lounged in the center of an air mattress inside like the queen of freaking Sheba, pillows fluffed behind her. When she lifted a pair chopsticks to her mouth, Marcus's own mouth went dry watching those plush lips close around the food, her delicate throat working as she swallowed. *Damn*.

Those lips would be the death of him. Mainly because Lily refused to let him close enough to get a taste.

"Mmm. Dragon roll," Clive said, snapping Marcus out of a fantasy that had begun brewing. "Do you think she went to Sushi Café? I love when they throw in a free crab rangoon."

"Unbelievable," Marcus grumbled.

The soft bluish glow that lit her face came from the computer tablet on her lap. It must've been tuned in to something funny. She tossed her head back and laughed, and he felt a punishing jolt of attraction as he watched her—the same unrelenting attraction he felt for her at work. Made no sense. He'd asked her out. She'd said no. He'd been shot down plenty of times, and typically bounced back quickly. He'd bounced back, or so he thought, but dating other women seemed…wrong with Lily around. Which made no fucking sense whatsoever.

"Yes, she looks truly terrified," Clive said, chuckling again.

"That's why I brought these." Marcus dropped the duffel bag at his feet.

"You don't think that's a tad against the rules?"

"I think all is fair in love and war and hard-won trips to islands."

Clive scrubbed a hand over his sandy blond hair and shook his head. "I don't get it, man. If you want a date with her so badly, why don't you just ask her out?"

Well. Shit. Was he this transparent? Marcus shot him a look. "What are you talking about?" He tried really hard to make it sound like he was shocked, or like Clive was barking up the wrong tree, but his voice came out thin and a little guilty.

Damn. It.

Clive grinned knowingly. "Yeah. I kind of figured out you liked her, like, a millennia ago."

Marcus accepted defeat, dropping the innocent act and glad for it. He was a horrible actor. "Does Joanie know?"

"No, man." He clapped Marcus on the back.

Relief.

"I asked her out once," Marcus admitted.

"No way. Lily turned down *the* Marcus Black?"

"Shut up."

Clive laughed. At his expense, if he had to guess. "So, ask

her again. She didn't know you then."

Yeah, well, she knew him now. And practically hated him. Or...not hated him. But she had his number...along with way too many women in Fantom who continued to call and leave him voicemails asking him for "one more date." Life would be easier if he could hook up with one of them... or several of them. But the dates with anyone other than Lily only left him feeling empty.

Which he did not understand. Thinking with his dick had worked fine and dandy up until he met the infuriating redhead. And now he was like some sort of lovesick puppy. And if that wasn't pathetic enough, now his best friend knew.

"Just stick with the plan, Clive." He was not talking about this. Not now. Not ever.

His buddy rolled a shoulder, unfazed as usual. It was impossible to intimidate the guy who'd known him since he was a gangly thirteen-year-old.

"I don't know, man." Clive looked through the window at Lily again. "You may not be able to scare her off, costumes or no."

"She's a prima donna." Marcus admired the wave of her long hair, and the open, inviting smile on her face, even in the dimness. God. He was screwed. May as well return his man card along with his balls on a keychain. Some playboy he'd turned out to be. "The moment she breaks a nail, she's out of there," he grumbled, his insult not sounding the least bit genuine.

Harmless insults had become the norm between him and Lily over the two and a half years they'd worked to-gether. He used to do it to get her to sling one back at him, because he loved the feisty spark that lit her eyes when she was busting his balls. She'd answered the call, mouthing off to him with fervor. But really, he'd never been able to truly relegate her to role of prima donna or diva.

First of all, it wasn't true. She worked as hard, if not harder, than any of them. She cared about her work, and she was a perfectionist who often achieved her goals. Secondly, he had gone from simply thinking she was sexy to respecting the hell out of her. His admiration for her work trumped the admiration he had for her sweet backside. And that was *bad*. He didn't want to change. Liked his eat-and-run style with women. Liked being the cad who kept things simple. But Lily... Nothing kept her from his mind. Not other women, not sex with other women... Nothing.

Resistance was futile.

"She's hardier than she looks," Clive said in her defense. "You remember the breakup with Andy."

Marcus ground his molars at the mention of Andy Lipnicky, King of the Douchebags. He didn't deserve someone as smart and funny and attractive as Lily McIntire. Marcus didn't think he deserved her, either, but he'd at least like the chance to prove himself. He'd burned that bridge by asking her out too soon...and had followed it up by severely bending the rules of the new account contest and taking the win for himself. Not his brightest move.

"She's a princess." But she wasn't. And even Marcus could hear the lack of conviction in his words. Wednesday night he'd had been shocked to learn that she was coming out to celebrate with them. It was the first time he'd ever been around her outside of work or an offsite meeting. It was like she purposefully avoided hanging out anywhere he was unless it was at work. He knew she had a social life, was dating a guy with a big nose and a stupid hybrid car, but he doubted she'd ever been to a rundown pub with a bartender named Curly. He'd looked forward to her reaction to the Shot Spot, where Marcus was a regular. Surely, Lily would turn tail and flee the moment she laid eyes on the fleet of mismatched chairs, and got a whiff of the smell of stale beer permeating the air.

So. He'd *thought* he knew what to expect when she strode in behind Joanie and Clive on Wednesday night, looking out of place in her fitted blazer, her heels sticking to the tacky linoleum. Instead, when she'd spotted him, she'd flipped her strawberry-blond hair over one shoulder and sent him a derisive look down that pert little nose of hers. About then, he'd given her a smile of bald admiration and made it his evening's mission to get her hammered.

He'd seen Lily in control, competitive, and icy, but never sloppy and unkempt. He'd fill his tab with as many frou-frou girlie drinks like purple hooters or buttery nipples as she could drink, then kick back and enjoy the show. He'd like to see the rigidity slide out of her spine, maybe get one of those loose laughs she liked to give him every once in a while when she let her guard down. Then he'd ordered a tequila shot and she held up two fingers.

"You drink tequila?" He'd been unable to hide his shock.

"No, but we are celebrating, right?" Ah, Lily the competitor, alive and well.

She'd arched a reddish brow and his thoughts had dropped to her skirt and into the gutter. Did the carpet match the drapes? God. What he'd give to know the answer to that question.

He'd eased her into the shot using old school salt-and-lime training wheels rather than just chucking the tequila back like he normally did. She'd followed his lead when he licked the salt and sucked the lime, while he'd taken a bit too much pleasure in watching her pink tongue lap the granules from her hand. And when her perfectly glossed lips wrapped around the lime wedge, he'd had a stern talking-to with the parts of him residing south of his belt buckle.

Pain in the ass, he'd reminded himself, tossing back his second shot. But that thought brought with it reminders of the way her skirt rounded snugly over her perfect butt each time she bent over to take her turn at the pool table.

He'd sparred with her all evening, figuring arguing would keep the hound in his pants at bay. But each time he jabbed, she'd had a sassy comeback. He couldn't help but admire her for it. Like he admired her at work. He'd always known she had talent—no one gave a confident presentation like Lily—but he hadn't known until that night that she could be so much damn fun.

Clive's cell phone rang to the tune of Marvin Gaye. Marcus dragged him down from the window and out of sight, scowling over at him as he answered. It was Joanie's ringtone. Clive shrugged an apology and answered with a hushed *hello*. Marcus gave him another pointed glare before risking peeking into the house again.

Lily must not have heard the sound, her attention focused on the screen in her lap. And she was drinking—good God, was that *wine*? He should have made more rules. Limited her to only the most basic provisions like water and bread. And maybe some peanut butter. Protein was important.

His frown deepened. She'd be a lot harder to spook while pleasantly buzzed on red wine, her stomach full of gourmet food. "I'm screwed," he grumbled.

"So am I." Clive waggled his phone. "Gotta go."

"Why? Wife gonna ground you if you don't?" He sent his friend a smug smile.

Clive shot him a self-assured grin of his own. "Joanie called to tell me she's drawing a very hot bath, lighting candles, and—"

"Fine," Marcus growled under his breath, not wanting to hear any more. "Wuss."

Clive clapped Marcus's shoulder. "Let's go, man. You wouldn't have won anyway. And hey, maybe she'll take pity on you and invite you to Hawaii with her. There *are* two tickets."

The image of Lily in a white bikini, pale, freckled skin on display, tiny triangles covering her most sensitive parts while she splashed in clear blue water, flooded his brain. He'd just lapsed into a daydream about applying sunscreen to every inch of her smooth, fair back when he noticed Clive heading down the hill. His buddy raised his arms as if to ask, *are you coming?*

Marcus waved him off, annoyed that Lily now crashed his waking dreams in addition to the pornographic ones he had while asleep. He returned to his perch by the window.

Clive trekked back to Marcus, tripping over a branch and stumbling. He was more *Mr. Bean* than *Crouching Tiger Hidden Dragon*. Stealthy, his friend was not.

"Are you nuts?" Clive asked. "How are you getting home if I don't drive you?"

"It's *Hawaii*." And he wasn't planning on handing it over without a fight. Lily hadn't exactly been competing fair. She'd forced his hand into convincing his cousin to redesign his coffee shop. It was *Marcus* who had sought out the senior living center on Merchant Boulevard. It was *his* sunroom design that Margaret Beckham had originally chosen, *his* suggestion to add five hundred square feet to the already sprawling grounds of Sunny Acres Retirement Home. It should have been the winning account...in theory.

But when Margaret stopped in to query about extras, Marcus's idea for a patio redesign fell flat. Meanwhile, Lily swooped in and suggested a koi pond and a greenhouse, and Margaret had been wooed by the idea of fish and plants. Just like that, *boom,* she locked down the contract.

Now that he thought it through again, Lily might have *saved* the damn contract.

Still. It was a tick for her column, and he was one shy. He'd done what it took. But her calling him out on "cheating" to win Hawaii was almost as funny as believing she'd survive the night in the mansion and succeed in taking it from him.

Not. Happening.

"How are you getting home, Black?" Clive repeated with a frown.

"Gee, Dad, worried about me?"

"Jerk." But his friend was smiling. Clive backed away, then halfway down the hill, called in an exaggerated whisper, "Let me know how it goes!"

Marcus waved him off.

After Clive lumbered down to where he'd parked the car at the base of the hill and reversed down the street, headlights extinguished, Marcus turned and unzipped the bag at his feet. He wasn't worried about being stranded on the grounds. Once he boogeymanned Lily from the house, he was fairly certain he could coerce her into giving him a ride home. Since she understood the nature of their battle better than anyone, she probably expected him to do something juvenile to win.

He smiled. *Challenge accepted.*

He'd have to try really hard not to rub in the fact that she'd be on his arm at the design dinner this year. She may do it with a look of contempt on her face, but she'd do it. Lily McIntire wasn't the type of woman to renege on a bet.

It'd be good for him to be seen with someone as smart and design savvy as her. He was aware of his playboy reputation and the assumption that he relied heavily on his charm to make his way in this industry. But while he'd never had a problem landing a date, having just any woman warming his arm for the evening didn't hold the appeal it once had.

No, this year he'd rather have Lily at his side. And the no-panties thing would be a plus. God, that'd drive him insane, her sitting next to him at the table wearing nothing under her short dress. Not because he'd never been with a girl who went commando, but because he'd bet prim and proper Lily had never, not once in her life, eschewed the common decency of wearing undergarments. And her doing it for him? That was worth fighting for even if he didn't want to go to Hawaii.

If pressed, he'd admit there was more to it than getting her out of her panties. Her ease in social situations would put him at ease. Especially this year. How the hell was he supposed to graciously accept a Designer of the Year award when he'd be surrounded by several hundred more qualified designers? He could hold a pencil and talk anyone into anything, but...*Designer of the Year*?

Part of him suspected this awards dinner was the ultimate

practical joke to get him back for the pranks he'd played on his coworkers over the years. If it wasn't a practical joke, well…that was worse. Because then he'd be expected to give a meaningful speech about his early influences, his process, his—

God.

The speech.

Just picturing the podium at the center of the room, imagining the white-hot lights beating down on him from overhead, caused his brow to bead with sweat. He pulled at the collar of his favorite T-shirt and imagined a noose-like bowtie knotted at the front of his neck. How was he going to stand in front of five hundred of his colleagues and not die on the spot when just *thinking* about the acceptance speech made him break out in hives?

A hooting owl snapped him back to the present. He could worry about the speech later. Right now, he had one mission. He knelt and dug through the costumes until his hand landed on the perfect one.

He pulled the covering over his face and listened to his breath echo behind the mask.

His mission was simple. His target clear.

Scare Lily McIntire out of the house, and win the date he'd wanted since the moment he laid eyes on her.

Chapter Four

Lily folded the cover over her iPad and strained to listen to the silence hanging in the room. She swore she'd just heard something.

A voice.

Not necessarily, she thought with a shiver. She'd spent the last half hour streaming an episode of *Friends*. Maybe she'd confused the voice on her computer with the voice still echoing inside her skull.

She turned to face the staircase. The room was swathed in darkness save for the circle of light her little lantern cast around the bed. In front of her, the grainy shape of the stairs rose up to the ominous upper floor, but the ceiling kept her from being able to see the landing. She'd spied it earlier, though, and knew there was nothing beyond the top step besides a yawning, cavernous hole. Just imagining the murky darkness made her want to curl up in that warm puddle of light and scrunch her eyes closed.

Maybe you imagined the voice.

It seemed to have come from behind her. *Right* behind her. A chill clipped its way down her spine, ticking every vertebra along the way. The hair on her arms stood on end. She tried, and failed, to convince herself she hadn't heard a voice. A voice that had spoken one word, a word now etched in her memory like hieroglyphics.

Go.

She rose from the air mattress slowly, intentionally, her eyes tracking from the staircase to the closed front door. The urge to obey the unseen entity's command, and bolt outside as fast as her Sketchers would carry her, was strong. But the practical half of her brain—the half logical enough to know a howl of wind could have masked itself as a two-letter word—kept her rooted to the floor.

Blood pounded her eardrums as she pulled her shoulders back and attempted to listen past her jackhammering heart and jagged breaths. She watched the stairs until her eyes blurred and her forehead broke into a sweat. *Come on. I know I heard it.*

An untimely chime from her phone made her yip. She slapped a palm over her mouth to staunch the pathetic sound and pulled the cell from her back pocket. A text. From Marcus.

Of course.

10 PM. IS ALL WELL? SEND ME PROOF.

Bihourly photos were part of the bet. She'd promised to send evidence she was inside the house. A time-stamped photo from her smartphone would prove she hadn't snapped them all in a span of five minutes then hoofed it off the property.

She tapped her camera app, lined herself up with the mostly boarded-up window behind her, held up her middle finger, and snapped the picture.

A few seconds after it sent, a return text read: HA!

Weirdly, she could almost swear she'd heard the timbre of his deep chuckle coming from somewhere outside the house. But then, she was imagining hearing a lot of things tonight, wasn't she?

Two seconds later, her phone chimed again. WHAT'S THAT WEIRD BALL OF LIGHT OVER YOUR LEFT SHOULDER?

Before she could stop herself, she'd snapped her head around to look behind her. And Marcus must have guessed she'd fallen for it. The next text read: SUCKER!

The banter gave her a second of relief, for which she was grateful. So when she punched in the reply of ASSHAT, she meant it as a playful compliment. The light on her phone dimmed, and she tossed it onto the mattress and sat, once again facing the creeptastic staircase...just in case. She reached for her iPad, and then reconsidered.

If she *had* heard something, and if it were a real threat, she didn't like the idea of background noise. If there was a rabid raccoon chomping on the exposed wires, or a freaky opossum hunching its way across the insulation in the attic, she would like to know. Even though the only weapon she had was the plastic knife that'd come with her dinner. She really should have brought the crowbar in with her...

Most likely, nothing would happen, and she'd claim Hawaii with nary a hair harmed on her head. She abandoned the tablet and dug out the novel she'd impulse purchased. It was a romance, thank you very much, no Stephen King for her. No, sir. She'd barely cracked the spine when she heard it again, as strong and sure as if she'd said it herself.

"Go!"

Gooseflesh lit her arms and legs despite the propane heater next to her warming the air. Definitely a voice, she was sure of it this time. It'd been tinny as if being played back from a gramophone, but unmistakably feminine. Almost... forceful.

Her dinner lurched in her stomach as her eyes tracked to the stairs leading up to the inky beyond. The voice had come from the second floor this time. If only she hadn't made out the word so clearly. If only it had been some garbled, unidentifiable sound, she could've passed it off as the house creaking. But she'd heard it. As clearly as she heard her teeth chattering in her head right now.

Whatever was in here with her wanted her to leave, and she may have needed to be told twice, but she wasn't about to wait around for a third time. Knees wobbling, she kept her eyes glued to the staircase as she felt for her phone and her purse. The darkness upstairs morphed into more shapes the longer she stared into it, so she risked looking away long enough to gather her things. She gauged the distance between the staircase and the front door, inventorying the obstacles that lay between her and the exit.

The urge to run was strong, but she forced herself to step carefully. Besides, not like she could physically outrun a ghost... Which did not make her feel any better. Following the mental path she'd mapped in her head, she stepped around the air mattress, over the lantern, and skirted the heater. She'd come back for her things in the morning. In the bright, happy sunshine. She was out of here.

Her feet hit the porch seconds later. She ran for her car,

not bothering to close the mansion door behind her. Heart thundering, Lily plunged a hand into her purse.

"Keys, keys," she muttered, searching for the lost metal in the depths of her purse. *Don't panic. Don't panic.* But she'd already begun to panic—each time her hand encountered anything and everything *but* keys in her Coach bag.

A sound in the distance made her jerk her head toward the house. The faint light from her lantern dully illuminated the entrance. That was it. No screeching banshee raced across the yard. No specter floated toward her on a cloud of ethereal smoke.

She still didn't want to go back inside.

She upended the stubborn handbag and dumped its contents onto the hood of her car. Lip gloss, pens, coins, and various other useless items rolled onto the ground. No keys. Which meant…

"No." Her voice came out as no more than a tiny whine.

She was going to have to go back in and get them.

She yanked on the driver's door, then all three passenger doors of her cherry red compact. Each handle gave beneath her palm only to spring into its original position. Locked. *But of course.*

She rested her hands on the hood of her car and forced herself to breathe. "They're in there somewhere," she told herself in the calmest tone she could manage. Other than a preliminary sweep of the kitchen when she'd first arrived, the only area she'd been in was the twenty square feet in the center of the living room. That was good. That was a relatively small area. It'd take her five seconds to search, ten tops.

All she had to do was walk back in there and rummage

through a few things. Although, her temporary boudoir was strewn with shopping bags, blankets, and snack food. The spark of hope that had ignited fizzled. The keys could've been inadvertently kicked under the air mattress, tossed away with her dinner container, or balled up in the packaging when she'd unwrapped the fresh bed sheets. She'd have to do a careful search to find them. That would take several minutes. Minutes that might mean hearing or—*gulp*—seeing something that would forever haunt her psyche.

Dread pooled in her gut when she cast another glance at the doorway, but she steeled her spine and put on her imaginary armor. "You can do this," she whispered. "Just go in and—"

A flash of movement—something too tall to be an animal, unless it was a bear—moved at the tree-lined edge of the forest.

Hallucination caused by stress. She sucked in a deep breath, closed her eyes for the count of three, and reopened them. The shadow moved, the shadow of a man, and lifted a long handle with a curved piece on top. Then it progressed, that figure wearing the night, crunching over sticks and brush on the ground and coming right for her.

The scream building in her throat stopped short when the figure stepped from the trees into the pale moonlight. But the man's gait was...familiar somehow. More of a swagger than a lurch. And when he held up—good God—a plastic ax, and groaned what she guessed was supposed to be a scary sound, Lily almost burst out laughing.

The face wasn't white with black eyes like she'd originally thought. It was... a hockey mask. On Friday the thirteenth. Another low sound came through the mask, and she shook her head. The closer he got, the better she made out the man's build, and it wasn't hard to guess whose shoulders those were—or whose handsome head sat atop them. And since he was trying so very hard, and deserved a little pay-back, she decided to play along.

Pushing away from the car, she pulled in as much oxygen as she could and screamed like any good B-movie actress. A muffled sound that could have been her name, followed by a slur, came from the man in the mask, who unceremoniously bonked into a tree. "Ow."

Lily swallowed a giggle, ran for the house, and pretended to trip up the porch steps. *That'll teach him.*

The asshat.

Chapter Five

Dammit!

Marcus pushed off from the peeling bark of a big-ass tree he could not see thanks to zero peripheral vision in this stupid mask. He didn't mean to scare her so badly. Good lord, the ax was as chintzy as they came. But the sound Lily made was a decidedly frightened one as she trekked from her car to the house.

God. He felt like an asshole.

"Lily!" he called, the mask muffling his words. He reached for the *Friday the 13th* face covering his own and yanked at the strap. "Ow!" How it had wound itself into his short hair, he had no idea. He half-stumbled, half-limped, thanks to the welt on his shin from a misplaced tree branch earlier, and lifted both arms to attempt to untangle his hair from the strap.

Through the eyeholes, he saw Lily stand casually and dust herself off. As he came closer he saw she didn't look as scared as she'd sounded a minute ago. She looked, well, *pissed*.

Her eyes were narrowed, and practically glowing with anger. "Are you fucking kidding me?"

He held up his hands to explain.

"You look like an idiot. Did you think I wouldn't recognize you in that getup?"

He was sweating under the mask. "It was a joke!"

"A bad one."

He tripped up the steps to her and when he got close, she did the honor of unmasking him, yanking the disguise off, along with a bit of hair. He yipped and she snatched the toy ax from his grip, swinging it at him full force.

"Ow!" On the second connecting hit, he caught the blade with one palm. It squeaked. Her eyes narrowed further.

He rubbed the spot at the back of his head with one hand. "Are you okay? Or did you fake the fall?"

"Wouldn't you like to know?" She shoved his chest with her free hand.

"Look, Lil, I'm—"

But "sorry" didn't make it out of his mouth. She snatched the ax from his hand again and swung it with renewed vigor. She was a lot stronger than he'd have thought. Did she take jujitsu or something? She was going to maim him with the faux weapon if he didn't stop her.

"Lily, stop!" He snagged the toy and yanked, catching her around the waist and pressing inch upon inch of Lily McIntire up against his torso. She felt amazing. She looked better. Wild hair, narrowed eyes, and flushed cheeks… Though he was admiring her way more than the situation called for. Especially since she looked downright murderous.

In no mood to cuddle, she pulled away from him. "What if I would have believed you? What if I had a heart attack?"

"You wouldn't have had a heart attack," he said, not exactly answering her. He hadn't thought this prank all the way through, he realized. But since he wasn't going to admit as much, silence was his only friend. He gave her a sheepish shrug.

She held up the mask. "Really?"

"I've never been to Hawaii."

"Yeah?" She threw the mask into the front yard like a Frisbee. "Well, you're not going now, either."

Her dander was up, and the ire swirling around her was like a haze of pheromones his body couldn't resist. At the mansion's door, she attempted to shut it in his face, but he wedged his hiking boot in the crack, preventing her.

"Move." She glared through the gap in the door. Just so fucking gorgeous. Every angry inch of her.

"Look, I'm sorry." He needed to wipe the half smile off his face, but damn, she looked good tonight in black jogging pants that fit snugly around her butt, and a matching zip-up hoodie with the word "couture" emblazoned over her breasts.

She continued glaring.

"I'm a dirty cheater."

"And?"

"And…immature." He held his palms in front of him but didn't move his foot. "Let me in, and I'll explain."

Those blue eyes narrowed further.

"Lily, come on. What do you have to lose?"

• • •

Frustration seeped from her every pore, thanks to the man gracing the doorway. She'd like to tell him where he could shove that explanation, and the mask for that matter, but as her adrenaline ebbed, so had her fear. Not so much from the startling sight of a Jason Voorhees mask—she rolled her eyes—but the thought that he could have had something to do with the phantom voice made her feel much, much better.

She'd take her prank-loving coworker over a restless spirit or a monster wanting to shish kebab her.

Still, no reason to make this easy on him. "You can explain from out there."

He dropped his arms, licked his bottom lip, and bit down on it, his dimple showing in the moonlight sifting through the doorway. She sort of hated how handsome he was when she was trying to be angry.

"First off, I was only going to wear it long enough to jump out and say 'boo,' but the mask got stuck in my hair."

When she screwed her mouth to one side in disbelief, he half turned his body and pointed at the back of his head. "See this giant bald spot?"

She didn't.

"Lil."

She sighed. He may be competitive and admittedly shortsighted, but he wasn't a liar. She knew that much. Door open, she stepped back to let him in. He shifted his wide shoulders to get through, striding in and glancing around the room. "Charming."

She'd never seen him wear flannel and denim together until now, and she admired the way his big body filled out his wardrobe. He looked a little like a lumberjack with a budding beard, which wasn't a style she realized she liked.

But with him hovering near, she became irritatingly aware of the parts of her body that had pressed against his solid form moments ago. Mainly because they were still tingling. *Tingling,* for God's sake. She had no right *tingling* where Marcus Black was concerned.

She considered his presence, his admission he'd been trying to scare her off, and the voice that sent her running from the mansion in the first place... *Mm-hmm.* She did believe she'd found the source of the ghost of Essie Mae.

He ran a hand through hair so dark it was practically black. With the pale moonlight at his back, his eyes appeared almost the same shade. Before she tumbled headlong into the depths of those eyes, she stabbed a finger into the center of his rock-hard chest. "Turn it off."

He crossed his arms over his wide chest, trapping her poking finger beneath his forearms. His mouth tugged at the corners.

She pulled her hand away before all that warm surrounding muscle distracted her further. *Dammit.* He really was attractive, and the part of her that kept forgetting she was preserving her reputation and work ethic wished she could act on that errant attraction, even if he *was* trying to cheat and keep his trip.

"The speaker?" She sounded out each syllable and pointed up the staircase. "Or whatever you've rigged up there to wail and moan. Turn it off. The jig is up, Black. I'm not going anywhere." Mirroring his stance, she crossed her arms over her breasts, standing her ground.

Undeterred, he closed the door behind him and towered over her. She skated her gaze over massive shoulders, recalling the way they'd bunched beneath his T-shirt when he'd drawn back the pool cue Wednesday night. He scrubbed his jaw as if trying to decide what to do with her, and her eyes went to the forearms that had flexed when he'd slid the stick between his thumb and forefinger.

"What makes you think I *rigged up* anything?"

"So what did I hear earlier, then? A ghost?"

"Maybe." He leaned in to say the word, that dimple delving into one stubbled cheek and making her want to stick her tongue in it.

"Maybe," she repeated, but her voice was a thin wheeze. *A turned-on wheeze.* If that was a thing.

"Whatever you say, sweetheart." He sent her a wink, a devilish one, the same one he no doubt used to sear the panties off his dates. "If you're hearing voices," he said, stepping away from her, "sounds like I'd better stick around and protect you."

"Oh no. You're not invited." She wasn't spending any more time with him than she had to. Not after the crap he'd pulled tonight. He'd probably Saran Wrap the toilet seat next, or put shaving cream in her palm when she fell asleep. She grasped his bicep, intending to direct him to the front door and send him on his merry way. But once her hand curled around thick muscle, she left it there, his heat and hardness soaking into her palm. He cast her grip a sideways glance and raised an eyebrow.

Why, whenever he was this close, did he muddle her senses? She rejected on principle the idea that a man could literally be a chick magnet, but here she was, being pulled in by the inexplicable and, yeah, magnetic force. Her nipples peaked and, she could swear, pointed right at him.

She let him go, breaking their connection. She dusted

her hand on her pants for good measure. "I'll be fine," she said primly. "You can go."

The cocky glint in his eyes flickered, and his voice dropped to a soft rumble. "You sure, Lil? You look a little shaken." He lifted the back of his knuckles to her cheek.

"No thanks to you." She swatted his hand away. As long as he thought she was scared and not melting into a lust-puddle, they'd be good. She pointed at the door. "Out."

He snorted, clearly unfazed. "As owner of the Hawaii trip, I'm entitled to personally witness your attempt to win it, don't you think?"

Absolutely not. She opened her mouth to argue.

"Don't answer that." He turned his back on her and ambled into the living room as if he had nothing better to do tonight than be a burr up her ass. Propping his hands on his hips, he surveyed her setup. "What do you have to eat around here?"

· · ·

Fifteen minutes later, Marcus lounged on the air mattress while Lily perched on the opposite end, watching him warily.

She'd packed enough food to host a small dinner party. Which was *awesome*. It'd been hours since he'd eaten, and he was starving. It was an impressive spread. Sushi, brie, grapes, cherry cheesecake…

"Are those Corn Nuts?" He reached for the bag.

She clutched the unopened snack to her chest. "Stop eating my food." She was adorable. Especially with that little line marring her brow. Lily sat ramrod straight, her legs curled beneath her. Every so often, she'd cast an uneasy glance at the staircase behind him.

He suppressed another smile, deciding not to feel bad for the tape recorder in the upstairs bedroom. Yeah, it was immature, but it was Hawaii. And anyway, if she lost, she had to go with him to the dinner. The prospect of a date with Lily had forced him to new lows. Desperate times.

"May I have a glass of wine?" he asked with exaggerated patience.

She snapped her attention from the stairs to his face, her reddish-blond eyebrows slamming over her nose. "No."

"What kind of barbarian allows a man to eat brie without a wine chaser?"

His teasing worked. She smiled. Okay, not really *smiled*, but the corner of her lips twitched. Progress, considering a moment ago she'd been about to dropkick him where he stood. She filled a plastic cup halfway with red wine and handed it over, filling one for herself while she was at it. They sipped in silence.

"This is good," he told her.

She gave him a slow blink. "You like wine?"

"Doesn't everyone?"

"You strike me as a beer-from-the-can kind of guy."

"I am."

She rolled her eyes and sipped once more before changing the subject. "I didn't see your car out there when I was running for my life from a madman."

He tilted his head at her sarcasm. She smiled prettily for him, and he immediately forgave her. Such a freaking sucker.

"Clive drove me."

"Well, how do you plan on getting home?" She widened

her blue eyes, faking innocence.

He quirked his mouth and laid a pile of innuendo at her feet. "I thought you'd give me a ride."

She opened and closed her mouth, then frowned. "Well, *I* think it's stupid that you had Clive drive you here like you two were on some high-school mission."

He shrugged. "I didn't want to get my car dirty."

She curled her lip like Billy Idol, which should have been a turnoff but was actually kind of cute. "Are you serious?"

"It's white. I just washed it."

Why that infuriated her, he had no idea. Everything about him seemed to infuriate her. Everything she did only made him want her a little bit more. Ah, the cruel irony.

"Well, it doesn't change the bet." She reached for her phone to check the time. "Six hours to go."

Six hours to figure out how to get her to lose. Now that he'd been unmasked, he'd have to rely on the speaker upstairs. Damn, she'd called him on it, too. Smart, his girl.

This girl, he mentally corrected. Not his. *Not yet.*

"Since you insist on stealing Hawaii from me"—he paused to appreciate her flared nostrils—"you really should throw me a bone for the annual design dinner."

Her eyebrows jolted. "Is that a sex joke?"

"What?" He thought back to what he'd said and chuckled. "No. That's funny, though."

She didn't smile, but her pressed lips seemed to be slanted at a slightly amused angle. Progress.

"What would it hurt if you went with me?" he asked. "You go every year anyway. You're obviously not bringing that last guy you dated."

"Andy? How do you know?" A flash of hurt briefly

crossed her features, and he hated seeing it there. Hated knowing that dickhead hurt her.

"Are you?" The answer had better be no. If he ever saw him again, he'd flatten him. He didn't like the way Andy talked to her—like her very presence irritated him.

"No. I'm not bringing him." She tossed her wavy strawberry hair and met his eyes. "Who are you bringing? Barbie or Bambi?"

Ah. Back on the clock.

"Neither," he answered truthfully. The answer seemed to fluster her. She looked away.

"Why do you want to take me, anyway? It's your big night. The last thing you need is me butting in while you're bragging about how wonderful you are."

The barb bounced off him. He'd like to take her because it'd be nice to share the spotlight with someone who knew what she was talking about. Schmoozing with his peers wasn't on the very short list of things he was good at.

"Believe me, after my speech—" Even the word made him start to sweat. He tugged his flannel off of his arms before grumbling, "I'll gladly hide behind you."

Her attention was on him fully, and he got the idea she was working something out in her head. Crap. That made him nervous. He didn't like being carefully examined by highly intelligent women.

"Marcus Black," she finally said, her voice lilting gracefully.

Shit. He leaned back some, as if that might help him escape whatever she might say next.

Her pretty lips lifted into a smile. "Are you...nervous?"

Chapter Six

The question was supposed to be teasing, but Marcus didn't laugh it off or shoot another insult in her direction. Instead, he reached for her iPad and tapped the screen. Avoidance. Interesting.

His head-in-the-sand reaction was a surprise. There was simply no way this confident, talented, alluring man was battling a case of nerves over an acceptance speech. All he had to do was say "thank you" and talk for a few minutes about how he became retail design's golden boy. She'd have thought he'd lap up that kind of centered attention like a fat cat would cream. She couldn't quite wrap her head around the idea of him being insecure about addressing his colleagues. Addressing anyone.

Figuring his worry was due to lack of preparedness, she asked, "Do you have your speech memorized?"

"Of course." He looked up from the tablet, eyebrows drawn, clearly offended.

"Well, let's hear it." Practicing aloud always helped her before a big presentation.

The corners of his mouth turned down. He dropped the iPad on the mattress between them and licked his lips, distracting her for a split second. Because really, his mouth was…

Well. She just wasn't going to think about what it was.

Rather than turn her down, he surprised her with a gruff, "Okay. Fine." Then he rolled his shoulders, cracked his knuckles, and wiped his brow.

"It's a speech, Marcus. You're not signaling me to throw a fastball."

"I'm getting to it." He scratched the back of his neck, scrubbed his chin, and cleared his throat. She bit her lip to keep from smiling. "Ladies and gentlemen, on behalf of Cameron Designs and my fellow colleagues, I'd like to…" He trailed off and studied her. "What?"

"You're frowning."

"No, I'm not." He marred his brow further.

"Are, too." She made a peace sign and separated where his eyebrows met over the center of his nose. The moment the pads of her fingers touched his skin, everything changed. She became aware of the heat rolling off him and seeping through her fingertips, of his whiskey-colored gaze meeting her wide-eyed stare. Of the supercharged air between them zapping like a live electric wire.

She snatched her hand away, hoping her shaking voice wouldn't clue him in on her now-stuttering heart. "And speak slower. It might sound odd to your ears, but speaking calmly will put your audience at ease." She intentionally slowed and softened her words. "And you'll be more relaxed, too."

She waited for him to argue or make fun, but he only blinked and watched her in the yellowish lantern light. "Thanks. That's helpful."

"Oh. You're welcome." Being the recipient of his gratitude was new territory. She shook off the urge to blush…and decided to lighten the mood with a subject change. "What are you worried about, anyway? We're not going anywhere if we don't find my car keys."

But the mention of their predicament made the smile on her face turn sickly. She had searched the bedding and bags surrounding them. Marcus half-heartedly helped while whole-heartedly chowing down on her food. Neither of them had found a single sign of her missing keychain. It was like it had vanished into thin air.

"Just picture the audience in their underwear," she said as she rifled again through her purse, which she'd hurriedly retrieved from outside.

"Will you be in the audience, Lil?" She snapped her head up to find Marcus leaning an elbow on one knee, a wry and damn sexy smile on his face. "Because as I recall, if I win this bet, you have to show up not wearing any…"

Her pulse raced against her throat, and she had to work extra hard to be offended. "I mean…" She shut her eyes to recalibrate her brain. "What I meant was, it's easier to give a speech if you focus on talking to the people you know. Joanie or Clive…or me." She returned to digging through her bag, reconsidering. "Or *not* me. Someone you like."

"I like you."

Her heart thudded. Such a simple sentiment, but for some reason, the words hit deep in her gut. Mostly, they teased, but when they worked together, when they had a task they shared, she liked him, too. He must have thought her twisted lips were a show of doubt, because he continued to argue his point.

"What?" He gave her a tender smile, a rarity, and her favorite from his arsenal of expressions. "I do."

"Oh, okay." She tossed her handbag aside and tried to get back onto familiar footing with him. "That explains the plastic spiders you've been hiding in my desk since we made this bet. Let's see, one in my paperclips, one on top of my monitor…one on the glass of my scanner."

"I heard you scream from the other side of the building." He grinned, inordinately pleased with himself.

She shook her head. Marcus was a lot like having a bratty brother around. He dragged a hand through his cropped hair and chuckled, the flash of his white teeth offsetting the dark shadow of his jaw. Heat flushed her neck.

Maybe "brother" was a poor choice of word.

"I'm not exactly on your top-ten list, either," he mumbled, leaning back on his forearms. The air-filled bed shifted, and she steadied herself with her hands. "Can't even get you to act like my date at a company dinner without adding it to the stakes of a bet."

Despite the easy smile on his face, he sounded almost hurt.

"I— It's not that." What was his angle, anyway? Why would he care if the stuffy redhead from work turned him down? His black book was likely thicker than both testaments of the King James Bible. "You're the one who made it part of the bet rather than ask me outright."

He pushed himself up and the air in the mattress shifted

again, tipping his face close to hers. For a half second, she forgot to breathe. She wasn't sure what gave him the allure. The casual way he wore his hair, the mischievous spark in his dark eyes, or the way the lantern lit his face, making him look like a boy and a man at the same time.

"I asked you out before. You said you didn't date your coworkers."

"I don't. But that was before...before I knew you."

He watched her for a few long, sweaty seconds.

She tried not to fidget.

"Would you have said yes if I had asked you recently?"

"You mean if you asked..." She licked her dry lips. "Just...asked?"

"Yes."

"No."

He blew out a laugh, his eyebrows jumping.

"I respect our working relationship too much to risk it," she blurted. She did respect him, but that wasn't the full truth. The truth was an ex-boyfriend had raked her over the coals. Emmett had used the fact that they'd shared a bed to promote himself and get her fabulously fired. She'd been the brunt of the workplace rumors that'd come with the relationship. Her ex had accused her of lacking ethics, and the pompous assholes running Lawson and Becker had believed him.

Not that she thought for one second Marcus would do the same...but at the time she had been stinging from that recent slap. She hadn't even told him the real reason she left her former firm. So, yeah, back then, freshly wounded and freshly shit-canned, she'd taken one look at Marcus and concluded that the dark-haired, sexy beast asked out every girl within earshot. It wasn't hard to guess they had all said yes. Every last one of them. She didn't want to be one in a string of many. She'd had injuries to lick.

But now, looking at Marcus, she chewed on the side of her lip, wondering if she'd made too many assumptions about him. Assumptions that had stuck, despite her seeing clear evidence refuting them. Like the fact that yes, he used to date a lot when she started, but recently, his numerous dates had waned. He spent late nights at the office almost as often as she did. And when he came in Monday morning, it was he and Clive who talked about hanging out at the Shot Spot playing pool or darts. Hell, at last year's RSD dinner, his date seemed more like an acquaintance he'd called in a favor with than a girl interested in him.

Huh. She hadn't really thought about that before.

"You respect me. That's a new one." His downturned eyes threw her off. Had she ever seen this man with anything less than 110 percent confidence?

"You don't need me to get through the dinner anyway," she said, almost laughing aloud at the idea of him "needing" her for anything at all. The man was talent squared. "Everyone attending knows you're ten times the designer they are." That was the truth, and so was the next thing she said. "And you're twenty times the designer I am on my best day."

Chapter Seven

He waited for the punch line, but nothing came.

Lily tucked a strand of hair behind her ear. She had cute ears.

"Like on the London store," she continued. "I sketched the interior of that building at least eighteen times, and I never once thought to position the POS stations throughout the store."

"Yeah, innovative."

"Exactly. It was." She poked his knee with one finger.

The third time she'd touched him tonight. Interesting.

"I was being sarcastic." Feeling uncharacteristically humble, he added, "Clive helped."

"With the final layout. But he argued *for* the traditional placement of the cash registers lined up near the exit. You were the one who insisted customers would be more likely to make impulse purchases if they didn't have to traipse to the front of the store to check out."

He vaguely recalled the conversation she referenced. The discussion with Clive hadn't been a heated one, and not one she should remember so vividly. Which meant she'd been paying attention to him, and he hadn't even known. How about that? And here he thought all they had in common was that they disagreed on everything.

"You sound like you agree." The two of them on the same side of an argument was new. Intriguing.

"I do." She looked at her hands like she was embarrassed. Or maybe she wasn't sure how to handle them on even ground. He could relate. Compliments weren't their usual fare.

"While I praise you on your good taste, I can't take all the credit. The London account was won in the boardroom." He could picture her standing there, her royal blue suit skimming over her curves, her hair pinned at the back of her head. She'd addressed Reginald with confidence, all while maintaining a smile and including him in the presentation rather than talking at him. "You were amazing in there, Lil."

"Oh. Um, thanks." She tipped her chin and blinked, her long, sloping lashes hiding her light blue eyes ever so briefly. "That's nice."

"I'm not being nice. I'm telling the truth."

Her eyes diverted to his mouth, and she licked those soft pink lips. The look she pinned him with next absolutely stunned him. The pursed lips, upturned chin, the way she was leaning toward him the slightest bit… He couldn't believe it.

Lily McIntire wanted him to kiss her.

Since he had wanted to kiss her since the day he'd met her, he was surprised to find his initial reaction was panic. Instead of closing his mouth over hers like the stud he was, he reacted like a kid with a grade school crush...and play-punched her in the shoulder.

What. The. Fuck?

"Hey." He cleared his throat intentionally, still unsure what to make of his reaction. "I have an idea." *I'll abruptly change the subject so I don't maul you where you sit.* "You can, uh"—he scratched his neck and averted his eyes—"do my speech for me." He shrugged and gave her a cocky smile. "You'll be like a ghostwriter. Only you'll be a ghost*speaker*."

Wow. What a freaking reach. What was he so nervous about, anyway? *How about because the girl of your dreams is coming onto you?*

Yeah, that'd do it. And he'd blown it pretty bad that first time. He did not want a replay of getting shot down in double slow-mo.

The longing ebbed from her expression so gradually, he actually watched it go. Her heart wasn't in the smile she offered him, and he was hit with the strongest twinge of regret.

She focused on winding the end of the blanket around her fingers, steadfastly changing the subject. "Well, you earned the award, Marcus. I'm sure everyone there will be—"

A crash from the kitchen interrupted whatever good-intentioned compliment she'd been about to pay him. She scrambled away from the sound behind her and across the mattress, practically landing in his lap. Her grip on his left forearm was so tight, he began to lose the feeling in his wrist.

"What was that?" she asked in a hurried whisper.

What it *sounded like* was someone overturning a china cabinet and emptying teacups, dinner plates, and various other place settings onto the worn wooden floor. From his memory of peering through those windows earlier, there were no dishes in there. And the speaker he'd hidden upstairs to play voices was not equipped with the sound of crashing china.

"I don't know." He studied the dark doorway in front of them, now silent in the gloom. He stood and she came with him, still latched to his arm. He placed a hand over both of hers, trying to calm himself and his thundering heart. Not only from the shock echoing through his body, but also from the feel of her smooth skin. "But I'm going to find out."

She released his arm and half hid behind him as they stepped closer to the kitchen. He reached around and held her against him, keeping her at his back as he listened, his every sense on high alert. He could hear the wind blowing outside, the propane heater humming quietly at his feet, and Lily's sharp, short breaths over his shoulder. Other than that, the house was still.

An electronic chirp made her yip, and she clutched the sides of his shirt tighter in both fists. "Sorry. My phone alarm."

He turned and faced her, pulling her hands off him and holding them in his. "Wait here."

He was supposed to leave her there and do his manly obligation of checking the kitchen, but found he couldn't move. The way her strawberry-blond hair framed her cherubic face, the way her plush lips parted, made Lily much too tempting to turn away from just yet.

Gripping her chin between his thumb and forefinger, he lowered his head and placed a kiss on the center of her lips. "And calm down."

...

Earth to Lily.

Marcus disappeared through the doorway of the massive kitchen to confront whoever or whatever was destroying Willow Mansion's dishware. She knew there wasn't a single breakable item in there, but she'd heard it, too—the creak of the cabinet doors swinging open, the sound of china shattering into a zillion pieces.

She should be terrified out of her mind. Either nonexistent breakables had been shattered, or she was in need of a psychiatric evaluation. But "terrified" wasn't her reigning emotion. The predominant feeling was attraction, and it cloaked her in warmth despite the cobwebs and splintered boards at her back.

Marcus Black was an exceptional kisser. He had firm lips, the bottom one slightly larger than the top. His kiss was no more than a peck, but his mouth had hovered over hers long enough for her to conclude that wine tasted a lot better on his lips than from a red Solo cup.

Or maybe she was simply afraid. Fear and attraction had a lot of the same characteristics. The sweaty palms, the elevated heart rate...

The picturing Marcus naked.

Okay, maybe not that last one.

Marcus—not naked—appeared in the doorway so suddenly she had to blink him into focus. His face was drawn and shadowed, but her heart ratcheted up at the sight of him anyway, her eyes automatically locking onto those talented lips of his.

"Grab the Coleman." His toneless voice snapped her out of her fantasy of being kissed again. "You've got to see this."

She forced her feet forward, lifting the lantern and taking it with her to the adjoining room. He extinguished the small flashlight in his hand when she stepped over the threshold. Holding the lantern high, she swept the light over every corner of the room before turning to him.

"I don't see anything."

"Right." He relieved her of the lantern, his fingers brushing her bare skin and sending a trail of fiery awareness licking up her arm. "Don't you find that strange?"

She started to answer, and then realized he was referring to the lack of broken dishes and not to the way his touch made her want to purr. Which he couldn't possibly know about. *Thank God.*

"No," she answered belatedly. "I find it fantastic." Somehow the idea she'd hallucinated the sound—that they both had—was more reassuring than the alternative. Ducking her head into the sand wasn't her normal habit, but this place was far from normal. And if she had a prayer of not losing her marbles while stuck here, she'd do well to pretend everything was A-okay. They both would.

He lapped the large kitchen one final time, his dark brows pinched. His boots stopped with a soft scuffing sound in front of her, then he lowered the lantern. She studied his brown eyes, choked by thick lashes, and his ink-colored hair tousled over his forehead in the yellowish light and thought of the kiss. How he'd leaned in and taken her lips so confidently. She'd bet he did everything that way. Confidently. *Thoroughly.*

"Did you hear me?" he asked.

No. I was fantasizing about you.

"Uh, sorry. Zoned out."

The side of his mouth kicked up, and her heart hammered into her ribs like machine gun fire.

"I asked if you wanted to go back to bed." He waggled his eyebrows and tipped his head toward the living room. "With me." He affected his best bad-boy rogue expression. Teasing her again.

He seemed content to ignore whatever they'd heard. Good. She could work with that. "You're impossible."

"You can't get enough of me," he said as he followed her to the living room.

"You can't get enough of yourself," she threw over her shoulder, barely meaning it. She took her place back on the mattress as he set the lantern aside and arranged his big body on the bed next to her. He was quiet for a moment, studying the boards covering the windows in the living room.

"You know," he said. "There are a lot of old trees out there. I'm thinking the wind caught a rotted limb and brought it down." He braced his arms around his knees. "Lucky it didn't come through the roof and kill us."

The sound they'd heard, as clearly as they both heard Marcus's explanation now, was *not* a tree limb. She knew it. He knew it. And she could see that he knew she knew it. But he was explaining it away, possibly for her benefit, before her imagination could turn tail and run away with her on its heels.

Back at base camp, the sound merely an echo in her memory, it *was* easier to believe a story about felled tree branches. Denial was a powerful, powerful tool, and she had no problem using it to her advantage.

There was one thing she couldn't deny, however—his insistence on returning to the air mattress to wait out the night with her. He was practically handing over what she had come here to win. Why not talk her into leaving? Why not create a panic and drag her from the house "for her own good"? Why would he sit here with her when he had the most to lose?

Unless…

"I had no idea."

He still studied the windows. "What's that?"

"You're a nice guy."

Without moving from his seated position—knees pulled up, arms wrapped around them—he turned his head and scrunched his brow in contention. "What?"

She nodded and gave him a smile, sure of her observation. "You leaped out of this room and put yourself in potential danger to protect me."

"Whatever." His fingers tapped a distressed rhythm against his jeans. "I *walked* into the kitchen to check for an ax murderer for myself as much as I did it for you."

Her smile morphed into a grin. "You mean like one carrying a plastic weapon and wearing a hockey mask?"

He gave her a bland look. "Touché."

"What was your plan, anyway? Send me running to my car and screaming down the hillside?"

"Basically."

She shook her head. Maybe he wasn't all that heroic after all. Yet she was attracted to him. Which could only mean one thing: Marcus didn't have pheromones like normal men. He emitted something akin to a hallucinogenic drug.

The heater next to them chugged, whined, and died.

"You've got to be kidding me." She hit the top. Hit the side. Switched the dials up then down.

"Is this the way you usually fix things? Just bang on them until they're operational again?"

"Seems to work for the vending machine in the break room."

He brushed her hands aside and inspected the heater. "This isn't a glass box withholding your Mallomars." The Coleman winked out next, plunging the room into darkness.

He swore. She felt like swearing, too.

"I just bought that!" she said instead. *So* not *the issue*. She flipped open the cover on her iPad and cast light onto Marcus's face. It died next. Just went dark, when she knew she had 87 percent battery left.

"What the hell?" He snatched the iPad, and she heard him click the button ineffectually three times before blowing out a frustrated breath.

With the heater silent, the room black, there was only the sound of the wind pressing against the boarded windows keeping them company. Cold, howling wind. Odd. Something was happening in this house and it was so very odd.

Also: terrifying.

"Marcus?" Her voice was a thin thread. She sounded scared. She didn't care. She *was* scared, and tired of pretending she had everything under control. Here in the house, and outside of it, too. Being a one-woman army was hard work.

"It's okay." His hand found her leg, and she clutched onto him. Marcus's body shifted, and she heard the clatter of the exhausted Coleman as he slid it aside. He shoved the heater next before leaning to one side and digging in his pocket. He muttered a curse. "My phone's dead."

Her phone! Of course. She let go of his hand and felt blindly in the small space until she found her phone. She pressed a button and blessed light flared between them. She examined the screen. "Forty percent battery."

He took her hand and directed the muted light around the bedding. His firm grip warmed her arm, distracting her from everything else but the feel of his skin against hers.

When he located the flashlight, he flicked it on and off. "Save your battery. We have plenty of light."

Their eyes met in the pale light emitting from her phone, and she felt the air shift between them, vibrating with a different kind of tension.

The sexy kind.

"We should go to the road," he said, his voice low. His throat worked as he swallowed. "See if you can get a signal."

"I have a bet to win. I'm not giving up because it's dark."

And she didn't want to interrupt the heavy tension clinging to the blackness surrounding them. Despite the shadows pressing in on them from every angle, she felt like she was seeing a part of him she'd never seen before. Or maybe seeing him clearly for the first time. Tonight he hadn't been as selfish and cocky as he pretended to be. The way he looked at her, the way his features softened when his eyes met hers, invited her in.

"Determined to take this from me the way you did that last account, aren't you?" he teased, his mouth tipping on one side. Regret pinched her now that he'd effectively removed the sexual tension and turned it into the usual argumentative kind.

"Sunny Acres. You really want to fight about this

again?" she asked on a disappointed sigh. "You didn't have a contract with Margaret."

"No, but I sketched a design she loved."

Lily picked at an eyelet in her sneaker. The phone went dark, and she dropped it next to her leg. "She didn't use your design."

Somehow that truth came easier in the dark.

"Of course she did," he argued. "She added on the pond and greenhouse, but she said the room idea was perfect."

She shook her head even though he couldn't see her, suddenly not wanting to tell him the truth. Which was odd, because the truth—that Margaret had requested an entire redesign by Lily—made for excellent ammo. It was the kind of thing she could have bragged about the next time Marcus one-upped her. But she hadn't. Each time he poked at her at work, she'd hesitated to rub his nose in it. Why had she done that?

Because. Because of the look on his face the day he'd won the trip. He was in his office alone, slapping the tickets against his open palm. Then he'd stared at them for the longest time, shaking his head, as a proud—not cocky—smile graced his handsome face. In that moment, with his usual veil dropped, she had seen him care about something in a deep, reverent way.

His reaction had caught her off guard as much as it had intrigued her.

Of course, an hour later, he'd plopped down on her guest chair in her office and run down a list of things to do in Hawaii. *Ever been snorkeling, McIntire? I think I'll cliff dive while I'm there. Thanks to my handy-dandy new shed, I have plenty of room for climbing gear and scuba-diving equipment.*

A scrape along the boarded windows sounded in front of them and, instinctively, she grabbed for him in the dark.

"See?" he muttered softly. "Trees."

"Trees," she agreed. Maybe they'd both overreacted because of the environment. Maybe here, inside a spooky mansion steeped in local lore, everyday sounds were scarier than they actually were.

"Talk to me about something," he said.

Good idea. She'd talk about anything to get her mind off the ghost of Essie Mae. "Like what?"

"Like why you wanted to go to Hawaii."

Not what she'd expected. She thought for a moment. "Well. Like you, I've never been there. Plus, it's a free trip…"

But that wasn't really why she wanted it. That wasn't the reason she'd worked overtime and gone out of her way to sign more accounts than him.

"The truth is," she said quietly, "I really like to win."

His deep laughter tumbled around her in the dark. "Yeah, I get that."

"And I wanted to see if I was good enough to beat the best."

She sensed more than heard his head turn.

"You're the best." She squeezed his knee. "You're unbeatable."

"I don't know." One rough hand covered hers, and on a soft rumble he said, "You may beat me yet."

She sniffed. That may have been a laugh if he hadn't been touching her. If her heart hadn't been beating triple time. He slipped his hand beneath hers. Heat from their pressed palms lit a fuse that burned up her arm.

"Lily?"

She couldn't see his face, but she knew his eyes were on her. She could *feel* them.

A beat passed. Then another. He flicked the flashlight on, his eyes zooming in on her mouth. "Don't suppose you're scared enough of the dark to leave."

She shook her head. "I don't suppose you're planning on leaving me on my own."

A smile, then, "You might cheat." He tugged their linked hands and leaned the slightest bit closer.

"True," she breathed, mirroring his movement. "I wouldn't trust you if our roles were reversed." Inches from his face, she admired the curve of his top lip. "What are you doing, Black?"

"I think," he whispered back, his warm breath fanning over her lips, "I'm going to have to kiss you, McIntire."

Chapter Eight

The flashlight clicked off, and Marcus's lips hit hers hard.

The stubble surrounding his mouth scratched her lips, but he softened a moment later, giving her a brief reprieve to calibrate her brain. Unlinking their hands, he wrapped his palms around her upper arms. He tugged, and she went willingly, then sort of fell into him. The air mattress was about as stable as one of those inflatable-ball-filled rooms.

Lips still fused with hers, he laughed through his nose as he fell back, pulling her on top of him. Lying against that hard wall of muscle, she didn't think there could be anything better than being held by him… until he slipped his tongue into her mouth.

Oh, yes. Much *better.*

She kissed him back, her tongue tangling with his while her fingers found the back of his scalp and clutched at his short hair. The feel of him, the smell of him, the *taste* of him was all so utterly masculine, she felt feminine and delicate by comparison.

He pulled away, his breathing ragged, and she shifted against him, feeling the hard length of him press into her thigh. *Talk about masculine.* She rubbed against him again. Shamelessly. This was crazy, right? They barely tolerated each other at work, were in the least romantic location on the planet. Plus—

"Sorry."

Did Marcus Black just apologize?

Chest heaving, she stayed over him, her arms locked around his neck, breasts smashed into his chest, mouth close enough that his truncated breaths tickled her lips.

"Are you?" she challenged.

He tightened his arms around her and ground his pelvis against her leg. His voice was impossibly deep when he said, "No."

Palming the back of her head, he dragged her lips down and slanted his mouth to kiss her. She wanted to cry with relief. Shrouded in the darkness, hidden from the outside world, this felt safe, like in this sequestered place, she was free to do whatever she wanted. *Whomever I want.* And right now, being on the receiving end of this man's dwindling control was *exactly* where she wanted to be.

She took advantage of her heightened senses in the dark, exploring his body by touch. The soft, worn cotton of his T-shirt, the puckered fabric at the hem, his hot tongue still in her mouth. She slipped her hand beneath his shirt, fingers straying over an army of rock-hard abs dusted in soft hair. She trailed her fingers up his chest, savoring the width of him, the coarse texture of him, and the heat rolling off his skin in waves.

When he groaned and deepened the kiss, his stubble scratched her face just like she'd imagined at the bar. He nipped at her bottom lip, her jaw, her neck, until he found the hollow at the bottom of her throat and explored it with his tongue.

Every brush of his lips felt more erotic in the blackness. She was a prisoner to each new and unexpected sensation crashing over her body like the tide. The heat of his mouth, the cold, prickling sensation when he left her skin exposed to the air, the surprise of his hand snaking under her hoodie and shirt.

A startled gasp left her when his fingers closed around one breast over her bra. His other hand grasped a handful of her butt, and he hauled her closer, still kissing and suckling the side of her neck with his talented mouth.

His jaw raked against her neck, and he dragged his lips to her ear. When he spoke against the tender spiral of her ear, she shuddered. "You have the sweetest ass I've ever seen." He squeezed again. "And it feels even better than it looks."

The wet heat of his tongue on her earlobe obliterated her senses and froze the response in her throat. His hands continued their intentional exploring, the hand beneath her shirt leaving to join the palm beneath the material of her jogging pants. He molded his big hands over the silk of her panties. And squeezed again.

She started to let out a soft moan but his lips found hers, and he swallowed the sound. He pulled away from her with a soft *smooch* and smiled against her lips. "Do you know how long I've wanted you, Lil?"

He...wanted her? Her heart raced for a new reason.

She'd thought, since she'd shot down his advances when she'd started working at Cameron Design, that Marcus had relegated her to the role of his nemesis. Or maybe she'd relegated him to the role of hers. Well, maybe not nemeses, but they weren't exactly *simpatico*.

"You want me?" she breathed, surprise infusing her voice.

"Are you kidding?" He squeezed her ass again, pulling her hard against his erection. His zipper pressed painfully between her legs, and he sucked a breath through his teeth, a growl percolating in his throat. "You think this setup works for me? That I'd choose here, of all places, to seduce you?"

The word "seduce" intrigued her more than it should. Being seduced by this man, a man capable of epic seduction was... Well, it was awesome was what it was. She relaxed against him, feeling a surge of warmth in her panties and ignoring all the good sense she'd clearly left behind when he put his hands on her.

"Have you thought about seducing me, Marcus?" She nipped his chin. The growth on his face pricked her tongue.

One of his hands left the globe of her bottom and slid between her legs. Even through her panties, the swipe of his strong fingers made her shudder.

"Only every night after work." He licked the underside of her top lip and pulled it into his mouth. His fingers moved again, and she squirmed against him. "Some nights it kills me so much, I have to take matters into my own hands." He bit down lightly on her lip, and she felt her bones melt.

"You—you think of me...like that?" And hadn't she done the same, holding the fantasy of him behind her at the pool table in her head while touching herself? She loved the idea of them doing it at the same time, both coming with their minds and bodies focused on each other…

"God, yes."

He slid his fingers between her legs again, her thoughts ceased. She wanted him. But she always had, hadn't she? In the bright light of day, she could pretend there was nothing more to her than the driven, prickly, no-nonsense woman she showed to the world. She could pretend she didn't want him, didn't need him. Act as if a man of Marcus's caliber was of no use to her, didn't fit in her perfectly organized life plan.

In truth, she admired nearly everything about him. The strong line of his back and broad shoulders, yes, but also his unbridled talent and ability to take on a project with zero fear. But even if she'd been willing to break her rule against dating her coworker, she knew she wasn't his type. Wasn't blond enough, wasn't vapid enough. And she wasn't willing to sleep with him on the first date. Except…this kind of qualified as a date. And she was kind of willing to sleep with him right now.

Five minutes ago, technically.

"I know you have rules." He brushed his nose over hers, echoing her thoughts. "Care to bend them? Take me for a test drive, McIntire."

"Here?" she asked, stalling. *Here* was not the issue. The whole haunted mansion thing had faded into the background. She was a slave to her body's reactions, to the heat of his hands, to the sound of his confident, deep voice. To him. All of him.

She couldn't see his dark eyes, but she imagined their taunting glint, the wicked twist in the smile she felt grazing her cheek.

"What if... what if I say no?" She wouldn't. She was halfway to *yes* now, her body humming from his fingers teasing over the thin layer of her panties.

"You won't," he said, his firm lips peppering her jaw with kisses.

She hated that cocksure side of him. Only she didn't. Maybe she'd been mistaken, thinking his confidence was something to be shunned. It seemed all her girlie parts were cheering on this alpha male. He kissed her deeper, his tongue swirling her senses, and she fisted his shirt and began hauling it over his head.

"What if you say no?" She pulled his shirt up and gave him an open-mouthed kiss on his chest. He shifted beneath her, a groan low in his throat, so she tasted him again, loving the feel of his hardness, the tickle of his chest hair on her tongue.

"I won't." He pulled his hands from her pants, but before she had a chance to miss his touch, he was dragging her hoodie and shirt over her head in a tangled ball. Her bra went next. He had it unhooked and off her arms and, before she knew it, she was nude from the waist up.

There was a snide voice in her head pointing out how much practice he must've had at removing a woman's clothes, but it was quickly shut out by another thought.

Practice makes perfect. No doubt he had many tricks up his sleeve when it came to the female form.

Not that she had any time to dwell on her misplaced jealousy. A second later, he braced her body against his and rolled with her. He shoved a pillow under her head, taking care to lift the bulk of her long hair out of the way.

"Comfortable?" he asked against her mouth, then

quickly followed the line of her neck with mind-numbing kisses.

"Very," she breathed.

He licked a trail down her throat, and she fed her fingers into his hair, her hips tipping off the bed when he placed a soft kiss between her breasts. His tongue circled her nipple, and she let out a startled gasp, followed by a thoroughly embarrassing moan. That…was the best sensation in the world. He pulled his mouth away with a soft *pop* and moved to her other breast, taking his time to trace her other nipple with care.

She massaged his scalp, her body overheating as he worked his magic. Her entire body tingled. Her head swam. Had anyone ever turned her on this much with his mouth? Had anyone ever tried? "Marcus, *God*."

He smiled against her breast. She felt his teeth and lips, the cool air abrading her skin as he inhaled. Then he was climbing her body, the air mattress shifting as he moved. When he reached her mouth, he kissed her and pressed his hips into hers. She squirmed against his erection, feeling wet and warm, and so close to begging for it, she should be ashamed of herself. But she wasn't ashamed. She wanted him… Oh, how she wanted him.

"What do you say, McIntire?" His voice was an intoxicating rasp in the dark room, an anchor in a sea of black.

What would she say? She'd say anything. She'd say *everything*. She'd been taken hostage by the man's inescapable charm.

"What's the question?" she teased, knowing full well his intentions. He ground into her again, and she clawed at his arms, wanting him closer. *Needing* him closer. He wanted her to say she wanted him. Wanted her to admit that she'd been felled by his epic seduction.

He nipped her bottom lip and soothed it with one slow, hot lick. "Make love to me, Lily."

• • •

Dude.

Marcus wanted to hoover up the words that had just left his lips without permission. He'd meant to say something much more crass. Something teasing and kind of dirty. Not four vulnerable words showing her just how much he respected her. The last thing he needed was for her to see him as some feeble-minded man with a knee-weakening crush on her.

And he was both of those things.

He didn't think he was about to be turned down—hell, he was halfway to getting into her pants—but maybe he'd misread her. Plus, he liked her way more than was healthy. Way more than four out of five doctors would recommend.

No. Fuck that. He was getting a yes. There was no way he'd miss the chance to take her to heaven and back right here on this air mattress. Not after a fitful night of erotic dreams starring her. Not after he woke with raging morning wood he'd had to beat into submission—literally. And still he wanted her. There was no quelling his attraction for her. No stopping what they'd started. So, yeah, he'd get that yes. No matter what.

You got this, Black.

He lowered his head and began teasing her breasts again, pulling one tightened bud onto his tongue and suckling her.

She liked this. He could tell by the way she played her fingers along his head. An answering buzz shot down his spine and made his cock pulse. He drove his hips against her, desperate to feel the wet warmth between her legs without her pants in the way. But she hadn't said yes yet, and he wanted to hear her say yes.

Actually, he wanted to hear her say, *yes, Marcus*, repeatedly in between heated breaths, he thought with a wicked grin.

He licked her with the flat of his tongue and pulled her deep into his mouth. God, he wished he could see what color her nipples were. He'd bet they were burnished peach, maybe a couple of freckles around them like the cute ones dotting her nose. A high, keening sound came from her throat, and he drove his erection into her thigh.

"Will you respect me in the morning?" she breathed, her hands pulling his hair in every direction. He liked it.

"You're going to make me work for it, aren't you?"

She laughed, a throaty, sexy sound. He liked that even more.

"I'm a determined man, McIntire." He pulled his mouth from her nipple and rubbed his chin against it, testing to see if the roughness against her tender flesh turned her on or off. She clutched his head, a high, tight sound choking out her ebbing laughter.

On. Definitely on.

"The bet still stands," she told him, her vocal chords strained as he continued exploring her body. "No matter what we do for the next hour. And this…this exists outside of everything else."

His lips came to a halt on her stomach. She meant

outside of work. Outside of the world they inhabited when they weren't pawing at each other in a pitch black, purportedly haunted mansion. Because he was a man, and capable of separating his dick's pastimes from his workplace pastimes, it surprised him to feel a faint pinch in the area of his heart.

She wanted him here and now. Just not later. He didn't like it, but it wasn't about to stop him from fulfilling a two-year-plus wet dream.

"Of course," he said against her skin. "Back to normal Monday morning." Unless he convinced her otherwise.

Another rake of her hand through his hair sent him lower down her body, then she blurted, "Joanie and Clive can't know."

What kind of idiot did she take him for? He knew better than to ask. He stuck his tongue in her belly button and she sucked in a breath. "Say the word, Lily. We're not going further until you do."

Her palms on his cheeks, she pulled at his head and he climbed her body, meeting her nose to nose. "Promise," she said.

He wasn't a kiss-and-tell kind of guy as it was, but with Lily…he'd never brag about her to their friends. He respected her too much. "Promise, sweetheart. Now say it so I can get to the part where you scream my name."

She tried to kiss him, but her lips hit the side of his nose. She muttered a small "oops" and they both let loose a laugh.

"Yes." That one magical word was followed by the softest, sweetest kiss on his mouth then the almost dirty command, "Now get to work."

"Yes, ma'am."

Chapter Nine

She expected him to tear down her body a second later, but instead he lay against her, his heart hammering against her breasts. Or maybe that was *her* heart.

Tenderly, he brushed her cheeks with the pads of his fingers, his words gravel-laden when he said, "Say that again, McIntire."

She grinned. Why, suddenly, was everything about him making her so...happy? The *hot*, she understood. The *hot* was a given. But the happy? Definitely different. Good different. She arched her back and wrapped her arms around his neck, brushing her nipples against the coarse hair on his chest.

"Get..." She gripped his ears. "To..." A kiss. "Work..." She nipped his lip as he'd done to her earlier, stroking her tongue over the fullness of it before adding, "Please."

His arms tightened, his entire body flexed. He wasn't the only one capable of seduction.

Clearly their banter hadn't ended at the foot of the

air mattress. They were still sparring, and the pattern was familiar, easing them into the unfamiliar ground they found themselves navigating.

"I like when you beg," he said, clearly in agreement. He tugged at her remaining clothing, dragging off her pants and panties, socks and shoes, and dropping them somewhere in the dark.

She heard his zipper next, and her heart thudded out a hectic pattern, sending adrenaline flitting through her veins. This was really happening. She was going to feel all that hard male muscle up close and oh-so-personal. She heard the rasp of denim and felt the shift of weight as he removed his jeans and dropped his boots with one *thud* followed by another. The crinkle of a foil packet told her he'd been carrying a condom, and for that bit of Boy Scout preparedness, she would be eternally grateful.

"Pleasured by an ax-wielding madman," she joked, needing to temper her excitement.

A deep chuckle penetrated the silence and sent a flutter of feather-light tingles up her naked body. His knees were between her legs as he worked the condom over his length. She hadn't seen him, but she'd felt him.

So, yeah.

Length.

A smile she couldn't prevent spread across her face as his hands landed on either side of her hips. She wanted to feel him inside her, stretching her, the delicious weight of his body when he came down over her.

Moonlight sliced through the boards in the window, highlighting one of his thick, hair-covered thighs. He leaned forward and the beam caressed his rippling torso, the forearm where her hand rested. She caught a glimpse of his face next, and he gave her a genuine, sexy smile before lowering his gaze to take her in. Light crisscrossed her body, a slash across one thigh and the opposite calf. He moved his arm and the moonlight lit the red-blond hair between her legs.

Starting at her ankle, he caressed his fingers up the back of her calf to the inside of her thigh. Her legs fell open, the pulse between them a steady beat. Gooseflesh rose on her skin in response to the opposing warmth of his fingers and the chill of the room.

His eyes on the triangle of curls between her legs, he murmured. "*Au naturale*," not sounding the least bit disappointed.

She covered herself with one hand. "I didn't exactly plan on…uh…company."

"Move your hand," he commanded. She did. He fed his fingers through the fine hair between her legs. "I like you this way." He stroked his finger along her wetness and delved inside, slowly, deeply.

She shuddered.

"Lil," he said, his voice holding a reverence she'd never heard before. He slid into her again. "So wet."

"*Mmm*," was all she could manage while his talented fingers worked their magic at the *V* of her thighs. He added his thumb, stroking her clit while she made a series of nonsensical sounds. Then he pulled his hand away, and she let out a soft little whine.

"Patience, McIntire."

She wiggled her hips. "I'm done being patient."

He leaned up and flicked his tongue over her breast. "Your nipples are perfect."

She laughed. Out of embarrassment or because his compliment sounded so heartfelt, she wasn't sure which. Again she latched onto the banter that might help her find her footing. "I'm sure you know what you're talking about, having seeing a few hundred pairs."

He neither confirmed nor denied, only spoke with quiet authority. "Trust me, Lil, they don't all look like yours." Lowering his head, he took one on his tongue in the faint light slanting over her chest. He must have known she watched, because he spared her a glance, his dark eyes zeroing in on her when he said, "Delicious."

He licked his bottom lip, and then drew the flat of his tongue slowly over her again. She shifted beneath him, unable to stop watching his slow assault, unable to keep from pressing her hips against the part of him she hadn't been able to stop thinking about.

"I want to see yours." Her voice was weak. So weak.

"No," he said, not moving away from her breasts.

Hands in his hair, she wasn't sure whether to guide him or pull him away. She was dying a little, in a very good way. "Why?" Unable to keep from teasing him, she added, "Is it tiny?"

He made a choking sound and lifted his head. The dampness on his lips shined in the meager light, and his eyes narrowed as he peered at her through a million dark lashes.

"You tell me." His smile turned predatory as he nudged her entrance with his erection.

She gasped at the contact. *Definitely not tiny.* But she'd known that, had intended for him to answer her challenge. "Then let me see it," she said with all the conviction she could muster. Which wasn't much.

He moved until his face was over hers. Against her lips, he muttered in a low, almost threatening tone, "I'd rather you feel it." Then he pushed into her another inch.

The sound that came from her lips wasn't a gasp, wasn't feminine at all, actually. It was downright guttural. More like a *guh* followed by an expelled breath. Because grunting was oh-so-sexy. This was one argument Marcus was winning. *Clearly*. He knew it, too, sliding deeper into her and pulling a long, low groan of satisfaction from her throat.

"Have it your way, Black," she managed, her eyes rolling back in her head as she shifted her body to accommodate him.

On his elbows, he hovered over her, blotting out the light with his body. He slid in to the hilt and paused, stretching her, filling her.

"Lily." A deep groan reverberated from his chest to hers. "Finally. Out of my dreams."

The words penetrated some part of her she didn't want them to, so instead she moved her hands over his body, admiring the curve his rounded shoulders, the deep planes and lines of his abdominal muscles. She loved the feel of him, hard but soft, strong but gentle. And from the throbbing member nestled between her legs, she'd admit, there was *a lot* of him to feel.

He pulled out slowly and she wrapped her legs around him, dug her heels into his tight butt, and savored every inch of him as he slid home again. Encased within her, he blew out a breath and dropped his forehead to hers.

"In a hurry?" he asked.

"No." Maybe. For some reason, the slower he went, the more she felt things she worried she shouldn't be feeling. As barriers went, speeding things up was a pathetic attempt at having one, but there *had* to be boundaries if they expected to be done with each other after tonight.

"Good. I'm not hurrying." True to his word, he didn't devour her, tease her mercilessly with his tongue and teeth, or rasp her flesh with the hard scrape of whiskers. Instead, he kissed her gently, his tongue tracing her lips while he moved his body in and out of hers at a slow, drugging pace, each slide winding her tighter, causing her breath to snag. On a low, barely there whisper, she heard her own voice as she sighed his name.

He drew in an answering breath, and she waited to hear the quip, the joke, the dab of levity for the most intense moment they'd ever shared. But he only dropped his head into the crook of her neck and laid his mouth over her leaping pulse as they found their unhurried rhythm in the dark.

As his chest brushed against her, she trailed her fingers along his back, reading the lines of muscle and ridges of his spine like Braille, committing every inch of him to memory. If they had only these stolen moments in this pocket of time, she'd take it. She'd savor the hardness of him between her legs, his chest hair tickling her breasts, the sound of his breath, and the reverent way he stroked her temples as he moved with her.

Weight braced on one arm, he brushed a few stray strands of her hair aside and kissed her cheek. He skimmed his other palm down the side of her body, his movements unrushed, and she found the word "please" leaving her lips.

"Really, really like it when you beg." He continued to rock into her as his fingers danced over her ribs, along the arch of her hip, and finally dove into the curls at the junction of her thighs.

Once there, he did all the right things. He knew how much pressure to place against the most sensitive part of her, knew how to coordinate his thumb with the forward thrust of his hips as he drove into her again and again. It was a delicate dance he'd mastered, and she was reaping the rewards.

"Say my name, McIntire." She heard the smile, *the dare* in his voice.

"No."

He slammed into her harder, his fingers quickening their merciless pace. "Say it."

"Shut up, Black." Her voice was high and tight, her body bowed. She was close. So, so, so close. And it'd been way too long since she'd felt this kind of build. Self-administered orgasms were not the same as Marcus's thick cock and his artistic fingers painting her into oblivion.

Another thrust and she realized she had all the light she needed exploding behind her eyelids. Her body bucked. Close, *so close* to release. Then… he slowed.

She tipped her head up, her breath sawing out of her lungs. "Don't stop, please."

He languidly stroked her. "I won't stop, but I won't take you there unless you say it."

Her voice locked in her throat.

He stroked into her again at the same time giving her the pressure she desired with his thumb. "I have all night." He lowered his head and licked her nipple.

And Lily surrendered.

Head on the pillow again, she licked her lips and said,

"Marcus."

He thrust deep. "Again."

"Marcus," she repeated, rewarded by another thrust and his thumb teasing her clit. There was the light behind her eyes again. "Oh, God, so close."

She couldn't pinpoint what drove her wilder—the feel of his talented fingers playing her wet flesh or the slide of his body against hers as he slipped inside her. Or the fact that he'd made her say his name.

"Marcus, please." It was more a whine than anything, but he responded like she wanted him to. Pounding her deep, continuing his erotic assault, he pushed her to the very edge of control… then over. And she went willingly.

Her orgasm crashed into her with the same force it would have taken to smash the phantom china plates in the kitchen. This time it was she who shattered, splintering into a thousand pieces and flooding the room with her high cries of pleasure. And yes, his name.

He moved his hand away from her center and grabbed her hip, grounding himself and using the leverage to launch into her once, twice. By the third thrust, he expelled a hot breath against her neck.

She caught him against her, threading her hands into his hair. His entire body was hard and unyielding for a handful of seconds until his release. Then she felt his muscles relax and felt a long, low, satisfied exhalation fan the hair at her temple.

She wrapped her arms around his big shoulders, pulling him as close as she could. He braced his weight to keep from crushing her, but she didn't think she'd care if he did. She'd gladly suffocate under all of his delicious, sated weight. The thought drew another wordless sound of appreciation from her. "*Mmm.*"

"I concur." He placed a kiss over her pulse, which was gradually returning to normal. He lay there for a few stolen moments, lips frozen over her neck before he uttered a muffled, "I'm trying to get up, I swear."

Her quiet chuckle was cut off by the heater and lantern simultaneously kicking on. After so many minutes of near pitch black, it took a moment to adjust her eyes to the light. She blinked a few times, and Marcus lifted his head, locking her in his dark brown gaze. She didn't look away. Or maybe she couldn't. He was still inside of her, still filling her. They were linked in the most intimate way, his penetrating gaze holding far too much honesty.

She really had marginalized him, hadn't she? Just classified him as a simple. One-dimensional. Maybe because she'd needed to in order to keep her promise to herself never to be taken advantage of again. Or maybe she'd just found it easier to pigeonhole him as a good-time guy and never bothered to get past his joking exterior. But now…she couldn't doubt the vulnerability so clearly reflected in his eyes. He liked her…as in *really*, really liked her.

That might be enough to blow her mind if the sex hadn't. And it had.

He closed his eyes and held his lips on hers for a long, soft kiss while he slid out of her for the final time and groaned into her mouth.

"You won. I screamed your name."

He blew out a laugh. "I think we can safely call that a tie."

"That's fair." The air shifted between them, a sudden

awkwardness settling in. Gone were the easy teasing and jokes. Not after that intimate pairing. Not after the way he'd so totally controlled her and she'd so gladly given up that control.

Wordlessly, he climbed off her and rummaged on their shared bed. She rolled to her side and found her discarded pants, sitting on the edge of the mattress, her back to him to give him privacy while he disposed of the condom.

She was so uncomfortable. Not nervous exactly, but definitely not calm. They dressed silently, her unknotting her panties from the legs of her pants as he turned his shirt right side out, every so often sparing a smile for each other.

Despite the slight post-sex awkwardness, she decided she liked him like this. Open, but quiet. Sexy as sin on a stick. He stood over her, propping his hands on his narrow hips, his wide chest mouthwatering even hidden beneath his T-shirt.

"You know what?" he asked, his voice tipping into that lust-soaked tone that made her damp in all the right places.

"What?"

"I'm starving." His eyebrows pinched as if his comment surprised him, then he let loose a grin that squeezed her heart.

Chapter Ten

"I knew those weren't safe," Lily said, mourning the loss of her Corn Nuts. "I only ate a handful of them."

Marcus continued chewing, mumbled something that sounded like "a shame," then upended the bag and drained the bits at the bottom into his mouth. He crumbled the bag into a ball, crunching merrily.

She shook her head and made do with the rest of the cheesecake. "Where did the wine go, anyway?"

"How do you lose things when we don't go anywhere?"

"Shut up." She tagged him in the arm as she spotted the wine bottle on its side across the room under one of the boarded windows. Thankfully, Marcus had wedged the cork into the top so it wasn't leaking precious Merlot into the cracks in the floor. "Found it."

She crawled off the mattress, and he wolf whistled. She'd expected him to. Her butt was in the air, and she'd been waggling it pretty good for him. Shooting him a deviant smile over her shoulder, she waggled it again.

"Don't tempt me, woman. I had one condom." He held up a finger. "One."

She snagged the bottle, smiling to herself. He hadn't had enough of her, and even though she shouldn't, she liked that. Maybe because after sleeping with him, she'd found she wanted more. To learn he was as insatiable as she was a huge turn on.

When she turned to tell him that there were plenty of condom-less pastimes they could explore, a *bang!* against the board next to her head startled a shriek from her instead.

Before she'd seen him move, Marcus was at her side, helping her scramble to her feet and positioning his body between hers and the window. She had upended the wine bottle, holding it by the neck to wield as a weapon.

"Tree?" she asked. Desperately.

"I don't think so." The foreboding in his tone didn't make her feel any better. Neither did the fact that he shushed her when she started to speak again.

Another muffled *bang* sounded, this time from the other side of the house. "I think something's outside," came his husky whisper.

"Like what?" she asked, her voice strangled.

"I hope not people."

Her stomach lurched. Where she'd felt warm and safe in his arms a moment ago, now Lily felt exposed, vulnerable. And foolish. They were in the middle of nowhere. The danger lurking outside the walls may not have been from some silly urban legend, but from someone made of flesh and bone who intended to do them bodily harm.

He extinguished the lantern, leaving them in the

pale orange glow of the heater. He faced her, staying her shoulders with his hands. "Wait here."

"Are you crazy?" She clasped his arms, keeping her voice as low as she could while feeling hysterical. "Don't leave me alone! What if they have guns?"

She couldn't make out his expression in the dim light, but she felt his patient smile all the way down to the soles of her shoes. He opened her palm with rough fingers and dropped a metal cylinder into her hand. The flashlight.

He lowered his head and whispered against the top of her ear. "Lil," he started, and already the fear in her stomach was receding, being replaced by lust.

Jeez. The man was a drug.

"I doubt whoever's out there is carrying a gun," he said.

Oh, hello, Fear. Welcome back.

"Probably just some kids daring each other to run up and knock on the door," he continued. "Ridiculous." He kissed her temple lightly. "Who would come up here on a dare?"

She tried to smile, but she was too afraid.

"I'll only be a sec. Find your keys." Then he turned and walked into the kitchen, lantern in hand. She followed as far as the doorway and watched him fuss with the back door until the windowpane rattled and the door popped open with a squeak. Moonlight streamed through the gap.

He gave her a brief nod over his shoulder and walked outside.

Lily shielded the narrow beam of light as best she could while

Marcus did a preliminary investigation of the mansion's grounds.

She'd overturned her purse (again) and emptied out the grocery bags as quietly as possible. Although if there were people out there, it wouldn't matter how much noise she made. They'd no doubt seen her car out front. But if it was mischievous raccoons or hungry coyotes, there was no sense in broadcasting her whereabouts.

She held the flashlight between her teeth and folded the last of the sheets and pillowcases, repacking as she went. The keys weren't under the mattress, which was on its way to deflating thanks to the workout she and Marcus had on top of it. The recent memory would have made her smile if she wasn't so disappointed to find nothing beneath it but the leaf-strewn floor.

Stomach clenching, she looked at her phone, noticing the battery icon blinking at three percent with no signal inside the house. Daylight wasn't far ahead, but it was still dark outside and would be for a while. And Marcus was out in it. Worry crept in, but she pushed it aside. He was beyond capable of taking care of himself.

She scrunched the pockets of her hoodie uselessly. Even if the keys *had* been in her jacket, she was sure they would have fallen out when Marcus took it off her earlier. She turned to the kitchen next, on the off *off* chance she'd overlooked them when she'd investigated earlier. She didn't make it a single step before she heard a familiar jingle coming from upstairs. A jolly sound anywhere else…but behind these walls, it was anything but.

She had two keys. A house key. A car key. Because of her minimalist keychain, she'd needed a bauble large enough to help her locate it in her oversize purse. Last Christmas she'd found just the thing to tie to the ring—a pair of large jingle bells only better suited to Rudolph himself.

She went back into the living room, her steps slow and purposeful, her heart thundering. The bells jangled again and a rash of goose bumps leaped to the surface of her arms. The sound hadn't come from her purse. Or this room. *Or even downstairs*. It'd come from the murky blackness at the top of the staircase. Real, ice-cold fear snaked down her spine, turning every brave part of her body yellow. *How on earth…?*

"Find them?"

She spun toward the voice behind her, her open palm landing over her tortured heart. Marcus stood at the front door, his hand resting on the knob. He lowered the lantern and shut the door behind him.

"Must have been animals. I didn't see anyone out there." His brow creased with concern the longer he looked at her. "You okay? What happened?"

Unable to explain yet another mysterious sound behind these walls, she shook her head.

"Enough." He advanced on her, his steps firm, his voice an angry echo. She might have flinched if not for the unveiled concern in his eyes. "Enough of this stupid bet. We can walk to the road and call Clive from there." Snagging her hand with his, he started for the door. "Let's not push our luck."

His palm warming hers, and the fading fringes of their time together, almost made her compliant enough to follow his lead. Almost. She stopped, planting her feet.

He stopped, too, and turned his confusion on her. "What?"

The voice. The bells. He hadn't been around for either

occurrence. "Where were you just now?"

"Outside." The confusion morphed into anger. His mouth flattened into a line. "You know that."

"Do I?" She thought back to the mask incident. The way he'd been trying to get her to call off this bet from the beginning. The memory of how another man had taken advantage of her threaded into her brain and sewed itself to this patch of time.

Granted, Marcus was not Emmett, but she wouldn't be played twice. She tugged her hand from his. He had been by her side when they'd heard the crash in the kitchen, but maybe he'd somehow caused that sound, too. Maybe he'd planned to get her good and scared. Maybe...she thought with sinking dread...he'd planned all of it. Including the part where he got into her pants.

Panic radiated from her limbs. Surely he wouldn't... would he? She searched his face, growing angrier by the moment. Having been a sucker in the past for men with knee-weakening charm, she knew she could easily be taken advantage of again.

"It was you," she said numbly. "Upstairs."

It was the only explanation. He'd vanished outside and demanded she stay in here, which made no sense when she thought about it. And now he'd waltzed through the front door and suggested they leave. Coincidentally, just a few hours shy of meeting her goal.

"My keychain has Christmas bells on it. I heard them upstairs." She pointed toward the second floor. "There's no other explanation for how they got from here to up there." None...other than Marcus taking them when she wasn't looking and sneaking up there while she stayed behind to search for them.

"Oh, you think that was me?"

He looked pissed. She gulped but stood her ground. "Was it?"

"How did I sneak back in here, creep silently up a staircase held together by rusted nails and wood rot, jangle your keys, and bolt back down here and come through the front door?"

He made a point.

"Okay, maybe a trick, then. You have them and jangled them before you came in." She wrapped her arms around his middle and grabbed his ass, patting his back pockets in search of her keys. When she turned up empty-handed, she thrust her hands into his front pockets and felt around in there.

"I don't have them, Lil." He lashed an arm around her waist and pulled her flush against one strong thigh, as hard as the striking angles of his angry face. A muscle in his jaw ticked as he glared down at her. "But feel free to keep looking."

"If you don't, then how the hell—"

Clomp.

Clomp.

Marcus lifted his chin and studied the cobwebbed ceiling. She tilted her head as well, not that there was anything to see. And there was no mistaking what the sound was. Footsteps.

Clomp.

Clomp.

Clomp.

They finally ended over their heads, stopping with a final *clomp.* The silence that followed was a living thing, wearing her heartbeat like a cloak. Her breathing turned hectic, the hairs on her arms stood unbidden. And her brain fumbled for a rational reason for who or what could be standing directly overhead.

"Tell me you have an explanation for that," she begged in a hoarse whisper.

"You mean other than the fact that someone is up there?" His voice was quiet, his face drained of color, his lips thinned. Pale light was visible through a gap in the water-logged ceiling. The steps began again, blotting out the light briefly as they retreated to the other side of the house.

Clomp.

Clomp.

Clomp.

Then they vanished into the silence once again.

Both fists wound in Marcus's T-shirt, the words trembled from her lips. "I take it back. Let's walk to the road. Unless… you think it could be Clive? Did you ask him to sneak back to scare me?" That didn't even sound like something Clive would do, but she'd take the explanation. She'd take *any* explanation. "Tell me the truth. I'm freaking out here."

"Not Clive." He lowered his gaze slowly, meeting her eyes.

"Raccoons?"

"Wearing boots?" His eyebrows jumped and he was silent for a few seconds.

"What do we do?" She wasn't beyond suggestions at this point. And she believed him about the keys.

"See if your phone works."

The button meant to bring her phone to life only produced the cautionary beep of her deceased battery. The screen went black. "Yours?"

He shook his head.

That brought the count to two dead phones, a pair of unexplained footsteps upstairs, and one set of missing keys now in the hands of whoever...or whatever...was tromping around on the second floor.

Perfect.

He left her side suddenly, and she was alarmed to find herself alone by the door. She scrambled after him. "Where are you going?"

"Getting your keys, McIntire. Stay put." He placed one boot on the first step of the staircase and one hand on the railing.

She grabbed his belt loop and tugged. "Are you nuts? Don't go up there."

He turned and palmed her face. "Not nuts," he said, his voice hard and soft at the same time. "I just want to get the hell out of here."

So did she. Hawaii or not. But she really, really didn't want Marcus to go upstairs and leave her down here alone.

"We'll call a draw on Hawaii." She forced a smile that Marcus didn't meet. She guessed he was still angry about her accusing him of taking her keys. "We can bet something else. How about—"

His stony eyes matched his severe expression. She backed from the staircase to the floor, but his scowl didn't improve with her vantage point.

"Do you think I give a good goddamn about Hawaii?" he boomed, the light from the Coleman in his hand casting shadows on his handsome face.

"You earned that trip. You were *proud* to earn that trip."

"And Hawaii was clearly my priority after we fucked."

Her head jerked at his harsh tone. "I never said that." Only she kind of had.

"Stay put, McIntire." His dismissive tone made her prickle.

"If you go up there, I'm coming with you!"

"No. You're not." He moved up a few more rickety stairs. The backdrop of the eerie blackness ahead of him covered her body in goose bumps.

"Do you blame me?" she practically shouted as she stomped behind him.

He froze, then turned on her, glaring again. But under the anger, she thought she saw a flicker of pain, then what appeared to be concern as his eyes moved from her face to her footing. "Go back downstairs."

She ignored him. "You were the one trying to cheat. Remember the hockey mask?"

"Lily." His tone was a warning.

"There are things happening here I don't understand." The voice. Her missing keys. The crash in the kitchen. And what had happened between them. Maybe that most of all. "I'm scared, okay? I say things I don't mean when I'm scared."

His scowl softened. She was winning him over, she could see it.

"You can't leave me alone down here," she said, hoping to nudge him into a yes. "What if—what if something happens and you're not here to protect me?"

His eyebrows bowed, and her heart squeezed. He cared about her. She could see it, feel it in her gut. He came down to where she stood and extended a palm. She slid her hand into his larger one, the feeling blending friendship with an odd eroticism that had never been there before. She didn't mind it…or maybe, she preferred it.

"Stay close."

"Okay."

"No running," he commanded, his voice strong. "I want you to walk. *Carefully*. This floor is a series of trapdoors waiting to happen."

The boards at her feet were not all that solid, she'd noticed. They gave just enough to make her wonder if they'd snap in half. Comforting. Almost as comforting as the phantom footsteps that had frozen her solid moments ago. If it wasn't Clive or raccoons, what was tromping around on the second floor of Willow Mansion?

She didn't want to know.

She really, really didn't.

Chapter Eleven

Marcus's hand nearly slipped from the sweat-slicked handle of the lantern. At least his anger with Lily had masked the very real fear carving a path into his insides like a dull knife.

He hadn't taken her damn keys. Hadn't seen her keys tonight at all, in fact. He'd checked around and under her car while he'd been outside and found nothing. And he knew about the bells on her keychain. Made fun of her for it once at work—referred to her as Mrs. Claus for a week. While he was outside, he'd heard the faint jingling, too. It was the reason he'd double-timed it back to the house. He'd been sure she'd found them, had been shocked when she'd pointed the finger at him.

Arguably, that was deserved. He did rig up a speaker in the west bedroom to play a voice. He had stashed the remote with the bag of costumes near her car. But that she thought he'd continue trying to tip the scales for the Hawaii trip after they'd slept together pissed him off more than he'd like to admit. Did she think he was that much of an asshole? Or was it just that she really believed nothing had changed between them?

Yes, he liked to tease her, and yes, the pranks tonight were a touch too far, but using her—*having sex with her*—to get what he wanted was over the line. He would have thought she knew him at least that well. Hell, the last thing he imagined would happen was that she'd tear his shirt off and say yes. But once he'd started kissing those pliant lips, and she'd started moaning his name. *Jesus*. He couldn't think about that now. Or else his body would forever tie being afraid of ghosts to sexual thoughts of Lily. That's all he needed was a hard-on whenever he went to see the latest horror movie.

She stayed behind him off to his left, and he reached back to scoot her before she hurt herself. Shining the lantern on the step she'd nearly impaled herself on, he said, "Watch those nails." Then, because he couldn't keep from touching her, he took her hand and guided her around another rotted board with "tetanus shot" written all over it.

He had to get over this—the part where she believed the worst of him. But he couldn't help it. Dammit, it hurt. And he didn't do hurt. Hurt was for people who cared way too much, and he made a habit of not caring too much. Except where Lily was concerned. There, he thought he'd prefer hurt to never having a shot with her at all... *Damn*.

She was determined to keep him at arm's length and he was beginning to think he didn't share that sentiment. She might have seen tonight as a fun little fling to fill their time together in the dark, but for him, being with her, seeing her fiery reaction to his touch, hearing his name roll off her sharp tongue… Yeah. That called for another round.

And it wasn't just the sex—although, sweet holy mother, that was a freaking out-of-body experience. It was nice to watch her walls temporarily crumble. To watch her give herself so fully to him, trusting him. That's what had blown his mind.

As well as he played the part of the player, no other woman had wiggled her sweet ass into his heart as thoroughly and quickly as Lily had. He supposed it was his fault she hadn't taken him seriously. But it still sucked. Because he'd done something with her he'd never done with anyone else. He'd let down his guard. Completely. He'd been bare in more ways than one when he'd moved inside her, had imprinted on the scent of her hair and each soft sound she emitted.

Shit.

He was a fucking goner.

They reached the landing where the hallway divided. To the right, a series of doors. To the left, just one room, its door off the hinges, moonlight spilling into the hallway from the window. That was where he'd stashed the speaker. Guilt speared him, but he sure wasn't going to confess to that now.

Maybe not ever.

"Don't you dare say 'split up.'" She stopped mangling his shirt and flattened her hand over his ribs. His skin had been branded by her unforgettable touch, and he ached to sweep her into his arms again. He guessed if he admitted the speaker thing, a second shot would be out of the question. So yeah. Maybe he'd keep that to himself a little longer.

"We're not splitting up." Up here, his voice sounded hollow in the barren space.

She let loose a frustrated groan.

He opened his mouth to tell her he wasn't going to leave her, but she didn't look upset. She looked terrified, eyes wide and focused off to the side, white-knuckling the material of his shirt.

A floorboard creaked behind her. "That wasn't me."

It wasn't his speaker either.

Every muscle in his body coiled. He moved quickly, lashing an arm around her and stumbling to the nearest wall. He pressed his back into it, keeping her at his side, one arm wrapped protectively around her.

Even in the light of the Coleman, he couldn't make out figures in the shadows. He held his breath and tried to locate the source of the phantom noise. He heard nothing but the almost audible rattle of his nerves.

He was far from timid, but there was something happening in this place. And he didn't want Lily here another second. She clung to his arm, her grip chilled from a fear as tangible as his own.

"I want to leave." Her voice was as fragile as glass — not something he was used to hearing from her.

"So do I, sweetheart. Let's find those keys."

With strength he didn't feel, he pushed away from the wall, held tightly to her hand, and walked to the first of many closed doors.

He lifted one hiking boot and kicked the door open.

"May as well start here."

• • •

Holy Hand Grenade of Antioch.

Arms wrapped tightly around her waist, Lily scanned

the room she'd followed Marcus into, shivering as a gust of air sifted through the rip in the roof over her head. It'd been there a while, if she had to guess. The boards at her feet were decayed from water damage and there was a roll-top desk tilted awkwardly in the corner, one of its legs having broken through the floor.

Marcus inspected a built-in bookshelf on the far wall, shoving soggy books from the shelves while searching for the missing keychain.

A spider web overhead caught her eye and she backed away from it, and the fat-bodied black jewel in its center. Something squished beneath her shoe, and she looked down to find an Oriental rug, soaking wet, likely from last night's rain.

"Careful," he said. "Any one of these floorboards could give." His black brows arched over his nose. He seemed angry...or something. Worried? Uncertain? His emotions were hard to read. That didn't keep her from admiring the way the shadows darkened his face, making him look mysterious and sexy.

Again, her heart ached with regret for insinuating that she'd thought the worst of him. She didn't. She was just... scared and had lashed out like a cornered cat.

Lily took a step toward him. "Why don't you just say it?" she prompted. She'd feel better if he'd talk to her. Or argue with her. She could handle that a lot better than his silence.

He held a book open in his palm. He shut it with a damp slap and tossed it onto the shelf. "What do you want me to say?"

"That you're angry with me."

He reached for another book, avoiding her eyes. "I'm

not angry with you."

"My keys aren't being used as a bookmark, so I doubt you'll find them in there." She grabbed the edge of the book in his hand, but he didn't let go. Much like in the tug-of-war over the plastic ax earlier, his strength won. He dragged her to him. She allowed him to, stopping short of stepping on his toes. She relinquished the book, and he tossed it onto the shelf with the others.

She waited.

He watched her silently.

"Marcus."

"You think I arranged this entire evening to maneuver my way into your pants?"

She flinched. That was fair, and basically what she'd accused him of doing. But it wasn't the truth. "I wanted into yours just as badly," she admitted.

Despite his narrowed eyes, she felt as if she'd made a bit of headway with that truth.

He lifted his chin and looked down at her. "And?"

She felt her eyebrows rise. "And?"

He shifted his body so he faced her, so close that his broad shoulders blocked her view of the bookshelf behind him. Leaning closer, his breath sifting into her hair, he said, "And did I satisfy your curiosity?"

His tone was hard, his back rigid. And yet she sensed he really wanted to know. Was he actually asking how he was in the sack? If she'd had scorecards, she'd have raised a number ten.

In each hand.

"You want the truth?" she asked.

A soft grunt, then, "Why not?"

She wanted to go to him, hug him close. Kiss him again. Instead she hit him with the raw truth. "You left me satisfied, yet wanting more."

He cocked his head in the playful way he had. "Don't tease me, McIntire."

She'd chipped through. A feeling of triumph filtered through her chest.

His mouth hitched at the corner. Just enough to light the wry glint in his eyes. "You're not just fishing for a compliment yourself?" He was back to his charming, rakish, cocky self— so damn sexy, her knees went gooey.

"No. I know how good I am in bed."

The barest dent of the dimple in his cheek tried to form, but he held his expression in check. "Come here."

With pleasure.

One step should have brought her into the circle of his arms, but the moment she set foot on the rotted board between them, it gave way beneath her. One second she was on solid ground, the next falling, a shocked scream on her lips. Her pants caught a jagged piece of the floor at the same time Marcus gripped her upper arm and tugged her roughly to his side.

Chest heaving, she clung to him like a spider monkey, eyes on her sneaker as it hit the floor below with a sickening *splat!*

She thought of the legend of Essie Mae. The way she'd jumped from the second story. The way Lily could have died in this house, if not for Marcus's quick reaction time. She snuggled in closer.

He bent with her and ever so carefully untangled her pant leg from the broken board. When he stood, it was to back them another step away from the gaping hole.

"This is so fucking stupid!" he yelled.

She trembled, but he kept her tightly in his arms. She didn't think he was yelling at her specifically, but he shocked her all the same. It was possibly the first time she'd ever heard him raise his voice. No matter what went wrong at work, no matter what had Clive pacing and cursing in the conference room, Marcus was the cool, calm, and collected one.

His hand splayed on the small of her back, warm and gentle despite his body vibrating with anger, or fear, or maybe a combination of the two. She peered up at him, into his dark eyes, and his expression softened.

"Don't do that again."

She nodded.

He pressed her close and kissed her. When he backed away, she sifted her fingers into his hair. "Thank you."

"I'd say any time, but seriously, let's not do that again. You scared five years off my life."

She could feel his racing heart under her other palm and gave him a wan smile.

His eyes went over her head, and his eyebrows crashed down.

She was afraid to ask, but it turned out she didn't have to.

Jutting his chin forward, he gestured to the doorway. She spun around to see a set of bells, and attached to it, her car keys, lying on the floor. No way had those been there a minute ago. Chills skated down her spine.

"We're going," he announced, bending to lift her into his arms.

"Wait." She stayed him with one hand. "I'm not sure how much combined weight this floor can take."

Given the grimace on his face, he either didn't like her suggestion, or was upset he hadn't thought of it first. He hesitated as if trying to decide whether to listen to her or not.

"I can walk."

He took her hand. "Hold onto me. And stay on the inside wall."

They trekked as quickly as they could while watching their steps. Marcus reached the doorway and dropped her hand, signaling for her to stay where she was against the wall while he bent and retrieved her keys. The second he stood with them in his hand, a tinny, feminine voice said one word.

"Out."

Marcus was on her in a flash, bending and scooping her up, heedless of the splintered boards as he took the stairs to the first floor, weaving around holes and exposed nails in his race to get them the hell out of the house.

Lily held tight and when she thought she saw movement on the rapidly dwindling landing above her, she squeezed her eyes shut.

He set her on her feet and threw open the front door, shoving her out of it. "Officially the worst idea we've ever had."

She tried to come back inside "Wait! My purse." The air mattress, the lantern, and everything else could stay there for all she cared. But her purse with her ID and everything she needed for her life outside of that house was paramount.

"Stay," he commanded, darting into the living room. She wove her fingers together and refused to look upstairs. A second later, he thrust the bag into her hands, and they ran for the car.

Chapter Twelve

Willow Mansion faded into the mist as Marcus backed out of the weed-infested driveway and onto the main road. Lily didn't take a single look back at the place, but her imagination supplied plenty of images that went with the sounds she knew she hadn't imagined.

Marcus hadn't asked if he could drive, but simply piled his duffel bag into the backseat, her into the front, and climbed behind the wheel. As he took the ramp to the highway, nearly empty that early in the morning, she rested her head on the seat and looked over at him.

Determination set his mouth into a firm line, and one hand was nested in his hair, the other casually resting on the steering wheel. He stared, eyebrows down, and she wondered what he was thinking. Then, he told her.

"I rigged a speaker."

She blinked, sure she hadn't heard him correctly. He spared her a brief glance, taking his eyes off the road just long enough to say, "I found a clip of a woman's voice saying the word 'go'. I had a remote. Whenever you heard that, it was me."

When he turned to look out the windshield again, she thought twice through what he'd said, then a third time. She must have been too tired to be angry with him because what came out was, "But she didn't say 'go' when we left. She said 'out'."

"I know." He didn't look over.

"And the crashing sound? Did you put that on the speaker?"

He shook his head.

"And...the footsteps?"

He gripped the steering wheel and kept his attention on the road. "No."

So. That was alarming.

"Come home with me," he said. She snapped her head to look at him. He didn't glance back, but he did put one hand on her leg. "It's not a sex thing, Lil. I'd feel better if I knew you were safe."

She didn't answer, but clearly, she didn't have to. Ten minutes later he pulled her little red car in front of a house that, she assumed, he owned. It was almost...quaint. Cute, even. There were flowerboxes on the windows, navy-blue shutters against white siding. And it was clean. Tidy.

What she'd expect from a guy like him was some sort of playboy bachelor pad. An über chic lair filled with high-end electronics and slim-lined furniture. She supposed those things could still be inside the humble abode she was now staring at.

But she doubted it.

The wide hand that hadn't moved away from her thigh squeezed. "I'm so fucking tired."

So was she. And now that they were sitting in front of his house, she knew he was going to press the offer he'd made.

"Yeah," she said, her voice holding a nervous edge. "Scary." The house, the sounds, and the fact that she was very close to saying yes to sleeping next to Marcus for the rest of the night. She was pretty damn tired herself.

"Want to come in?" His tone was low, gentle.

"Marcus."

"I don't want you driving home." He lifted his knuckles and brushed her cheek. Her eyes closed heavily. As if it was decided, he pulled his hand away and unbuckled his belt. "Let's go inside, McIntire. I have a warm bed with me in it waiting for you."

"It's probably better that I go home."

He didn't acknowledge her weakly spoken argument, instead climbing out and rounding the vehicle, where he opened the door. He bent over her, unclipped her seat belt, and then hauled her out of the car.

"The manhandling isn't necessary," she grumbled.

He pulled her close to his lips, gripping her firmly by her arms. "Get your incredible ass in my house."

"Why?" She beat back the smile dying to produce itself on her face.

He grinned. "So you can protect me from the things that go bump in the night."

Her knees went soft. "Was that a sex joke?"

"Yeah." And now his eyes were twinkling.

"Fine." She shook out of his grasp, leaned into the car, and snatched up her purse. "I'll stay."

"That's my girl." He took his bag from the backseat and locked her car with the key fob. It made her remember the remote he'd confessed to, which made her surly all over again.

"You bought a speaker to play a voice by remote," she said as he unlocked the door and went inside.

"Going to bed," he called over his shoulder.

If she wasn't so tired, she might have argued with him. Then again, he did have her keys. She was having trouble holding onto those suckers.

"What about my missing keys?" She stepped inside and closed the door. He hadn't bothered with the lights, so she couldn't look around.

"I don't know how to explain half the shit that went on tonight," he admitted, dropping his bag on the floor and coming to her. "We're going to sleep now, and ask questions later."

"I'm not having sex with you."

"McIntire."

"Again," she said around a yawn.

"Not tonight you aren't. Come on." He lifted her, gingerly this time. Her legs felt as if they were wrapped in lead. She was crashing and crashing hard. By the time he laid her on a very soft mattress, her eyes refused to open. He undressed her, and soon after she lost all sense of time and place as her consciousness faded into dreamland.

• • •

In his bed.

Lily McIntire was in his bed.

Not an air mattress in a crumbling house, but wrapped in slate gray sheets, her strawberry-blond hair spread over a pillow. He'd put her in one of his T-shirts and since she was already out, didn't even get a kiss good night.

He'd crawled in next to her and slept like the dead. Which reminded him of the unexplained sounds in the mansion. What the fuck? He didn't believe in hauntings, but he and Lily had been in the house, all over it, and found nothing to explain what they'd heard.

It was as inexplicable as the heat sizzling between them last night.

Head propped on one arm, he stared blankly at the framed photo on his wall—a photo of Diamond Head Volcano in Oahu. He'd always wanted to see it, ever since he was a kid and learned about it. The ragged brown peaks offset an impossibly blue sky and turquoise water dotted with surfers.

He hauled in the first deep breath he'd taken since last night and looked at the clock on his nightstand. Eleven. Late for him. Even for a Saturday.

Exhaustion had hit him hard. He'd sunk into sleep shortly after Lily, barely slipping back to reality when she jostled the bed, he assumed to use his bathroom. He'd been unable to open his eyes. It was nice, though, the feeling of her sliding in next to him when she came back. It'd been a while since he'd slept next to a woman. If someone would have told him a week ago that come Saturday the next woman he'd wake up to was Lily McIntire, he'd have sooner believed in the Tooth Fairy.

Then again, he was believing in all sorts of things lately. His pragmatism had been given a run for its money.

He turned his head and studied her sleepy face, the way her lashes lay softly against her cheeks. The freckles on her nose. *Gorgeous.* His dick bobbed. He couldn't help it. Normally when he woke with a hard-on, it was with Lily in mind. With her in the flesh, there was no way to avoid it.

He remembered every sigh, the sound of his name as she called it out, the way she felt coming, clenching around him as he pumped into her. He grunted uncomfortably and adjusted himself. No way could he keep thinking in that direction if he wanted his dick to retreat to a neutral corner. And he couldn't exactly wake her up for morning sex.

Could he?

She licked her lips and stretched next to him like a languid cat, her nipples punching against the soft cotton of the T-shirt she wore.

Prob'ly not.

He did have the day free. Even hardworking Lily didn't go in on Saturdays, unless they had a big bid they were trying to win. But they'd nailed the London account, so there was no need to work overtime and weekends now. Still, it wasn't hard to guess that the moment she opened her eyes, she would realize where she was then make a hasty excuse, clipping away from him with that smart little walk she had.

Not what he wanted. He studied the threads of blond running through her soft, reddish hair. He'd like a cup of coffee, maybe breakfast. Wouldn't mind talking to her a while they lounged on the deck. Which was really weird. Because in the past when a woman was in his bed, his plan in the morning was to get up, put on his workout gear, and wake her up using the excuse of a ten-mile run.

Sleepy women didn't want to get up at five a.m. for a

ten-mile run, he'd learned. At the suggestion, most simply climbed out of bed and left without too much argument. If they stayed the night at all. Now that he was admiring the light freckles dotting Lily's cheeks, he tried to remember the last woman he'd kicked out of bed and realized it'd been a while.

He calculated back, recalling a rowdy Saint Patrick's Day, and then realized that was about the time Lily and Andy were on the rocks. Surely he didn't curb himself thinking he'd have a shot with her... A guy of his caliber wouldn't bench his libido without a guarantee...

He pulled a hand over his face, feeling the thick growth there.

Damn. *Had* he done that?

Lily stretched again and he couldn't help smiling. If he'd thought she was cute on her air mattress eating sushi yesterday, right now she was damned adorable with sunlight in her crumpled hair. Who knew she had those curls in the morning? He wound one around his finger as her eyes fluttered open.

"Morning, McIntire."

She sucked in a deep breath, a smile tickling her peach-pink lips. Lips he wanted to kiss.

"Where's my coffee, Black? What kind of host are you, anyway?" Her voice was thick and sleepy and she'd woken up busting his balls first thing. He shouldn't like it, but he did.

Unable to resist, he reached for her hips under the sheets and tucked her next to him. "Have an idea."

"Hmm." She nudged his erection with her backside and he grunted, his hand climbing her hip and beneath the

T-shirt.

She rolled over, the sound of sheets sliding over her partially naked body making him harder than he was—and that was saying something. Her light blue eyes slammed into him. Thought evaporated as his body took over. He flattened his hand on her bare skin under her shirt, smashing her breasts to his chest. He kissed her lightly, then deeply when her tongue snaked out for a taste of him. Then they were making out fervently, her leg sliding against his, a grunt low in her throat as she tilted her head to kiss him again, then—

"Wait."

Shit. He didn't want to wait. He backed off some, rerouting the hand that'd been going for a breast. He swallowed thickly and tried to see her clearly through the lust veiling his senses.

She slid her leg away and backed her hips from his a second later. "Um…"

Well. This wasn't good. Covering, he tried to avoid this moment by talking over her. "Right. You asked for coffee. Coffee and kisses. Always get those two confused." It was supposed to be funny, but the lame joke fell flat, deflating the sensual tension and leaving behind only tightened strain.

He didn't like it.

She blew out a small laugh, but he could tell she was uncomfortable. And when her blue eyes flitted to the side, then snapped back to him, there was a shutter there that made his heart sink—like she'd purposefully backed away, even though she was lying inches from him. He didn't like the distance, and she couldn't hide it. In the late morning sunshine, it was impossible to miss.

He'd seen a similar weightiness before, when he lived

with Annie. He'd been in a serious relationship a long time ago. He had thought things were fine. Then he woke up one morning, after living in her apartment for seven months, to a similar expression to the one Lily wore now. Their final conversation had started out with—

"Listen, Marcus…"

Fuck.

"Second thought," he said, throwing the sheet off himself and putting his feet on the floor. No way was he letting her dump him when they'd barely gotten started. "I missed my run." He went to the closet and pulled on a pair of jogging pants, busying himself to cover the moment—and his raging hard-on. "Do you run, McIntire?"

"No." She sat up and studied him a quizzically.

"I do ten miles." He snatched a long-sleeved shirt off a hanger. "Uphill some of the way."

"Marcus."

Yeah, he didn't think he'd be able to distract her. But he wasn't going to stick around and wait for her to finish whatever had started with "Listen, Marcus…", either. With an easy, practiced smile, he came to her side of the bed and lowered his lips for a kiss. "Hang out if you want, but if you have stuff to do, I get it."

"Are you…mad?" she asked as he pulled a pair of socks from his top dresser drawer.

"Not mad." He wasn't. But it didn't make this exchange any more pleasant. He got it—it sucked, but he got it. Under the cover of night at Willow Mansion, where things happened and no one knew why, he and Lily could be one thing. But here in the real world—in the glaring daylight, they were back to themselves. Coworkers who didn't sleep together and argued over who got the last crab rangoon at lunch.

"Coffee, you said?" he asked, snatching up his tennis shoes. "I can make you one to go."

She frowned, but agreed. "That'd be good, thanks."

"No problem," he lied, walking out of his room and taking the stairs two at a time.

. . .

Lily felt her brow scrunch as Marcus disappeared, leaving her wearing only his T-shirt and sheets. This was…strange.

Did he actually think he could roll over and convince her to have sex just because she was here?

You wanted to.

She did. Lord help her, the moment his lips hit hers, her brain went AWOL. And there was still a distinct warmth between her legs telling her she'd made a big mistake in pushing him away. And what was with that jogging excuse? Did Marcus really jog?

She dressed quickly, finding her clothes thrown over a chair in the corner of Marcus's rather spacious bedroom. The room was a little cool so she was glad she had a hoodie to throw on. She opted to wear Marcus's bigger T-shirt. It was warm from her wearing it, and she really didn't want to fuss with a bra this early. So, she balled up her shirt and bra, determined to stuff them into her purse. She wouldn't be here long anyway. She'd just head home and try to have a normal weekend. Clean the house, do laundry…feed her neglected goldfish. She'd have to spend some extra time with Bubbles today.

Sure. That's better than morning sex with the hunk downstairs.

She sighed, straightening the sheets and pillows in a sloppy attempt at making the bed. She wasn't going to think about sleeping with Marcus last night. Literally sleeping. Snuggling next to his big body had been nice, and she didn't like that she liked it. It would be better if it had been neutral and they could just go back to being friends. Sort of. If that's what they were. Acquaintances seemed the wrong label after last night, which was…intense. Proof was in the fact she hadn't thought about how she almost dropped through the rotted floor to her death until just now.

A huge poster of what looked like mountains in Oahu caught her attention. The picture was framed and hanging over Marcus's solid, dark-stained dresser. She shook her head, considering. So, Hawaii wasn't just another chance to win something. He really, really wanted to go. She smiled softly, reaching out a finger to swipe away a bit of dust from the frame. He'd had it a while.

"Lock up behind you, McIntire!" a voice called up the stairs. She walked to the railing and peeked down at Marcus. He stood at the front door, dressed, jacket on, sunglasses hiding his eyes.

"Seriously? You're really going jogging?" Now? Instead of hanging out with her?

But you don't want him to hang out with you.

Or, rather, she *shouldn't* want him to. She did though.

"How else do you think I maintain my sexy figure?" He gestured to himself—and yes, his sexy figure—and grinned to beat all. He was back to himself. Less intense. Less looking at her like she was edible. He'd either completely blown off her awkward rejection this morning, or else he was really good at faking it. "Stay as long as you like. I don't think you're going to steal my stuff or anything."

Steal.

As he closed the door behind him, she sat on the top step, her limbs going numb. That word acted as a palpable reminder that by cutting Marcus short before they went too far, she'd done the right thing. It was maybe too late to rectify what happened last night, but he'd promised not to tell Joanie and Clive, so really, they could go back to normal on Monday.

The last time she'd had a relationship with her coworker and earned a promotion, he'd gone over her head and accused her of stealing his design. Being this vulnerable with anyone was hard, but when an affair intertwined career and personal life, it was potentially twice as damaging.

She stood, swiped her hands down her pants, and went downstairs. As promised, a travel mug sat steaming on the countertop. She took a sip and found it was already creamed just the way she liked it.

Trying not to read too much into that, she tucked her bra and shirt into her purse, grabbed her coffee and keys, and locked up behind her.

Chapter Thirteen

Lily swiped mascara onto her lashes Monday morning and regarded her reflection in her bathroom mirror dubiously. She was supposed to be back to normal by today. Supposed to have forgotten that Friday night—going into Saturday morning—had ever happened.

She'd gone about her duties over the weekend, doing a load of whites and scrubbing her refrigerator until it shined inside and out. But all the while, she was turning over the fact that Marcus's house was cozy and homey, that his bedroom, while not frilly and girlie, did have the touch of design to it. Thick slate gray curtains matching the sheets, light beige walls, and his furniture all matched. He didn't have glass end tables or a wrought iron bed frame. No white leather furniture—no black leather for that matter. No, his sofa was a rich mahogany color with big, square gold pillows, the end tables flanking it of old-world design.

She noticed all of those things in her brief visit to his

house, and it bugged her she'd been so wrong about his living situation. Why this bothered her, she had no idea.

Yes, you do.

Yes. She did.

Because it made him harder to marginalize. She'd assumed he was a playboy. At best, a super neat freak with clean lines and monochrome furnishings, or at worst, living like a frat boy with a TV on milk crates and dirty clothes strewn on his bedroom floor. But his house was comfy. He was comfy. And the idea she'd been comfy with him was freaking her out.

They'd slept side by side in his bed, and she'd slept great—and after the night at Willow Mansion, she should *not* have slept great.

So. She drove to work giving herself a stern talking to. No matter what all her feelings were saying, her mind and instincts warned her against anything long-term. A workplace romance was not the end goal.

She and Marcus had simply had a consensual one-night stand. And while she wasn't as versed in the after-effects of hooking up, having been a relationship type girl up until now, she was sure Marcus would find his footing easily. Hell, maybe he already had.

She'd see soon enough at work. Too soon, she thought with sinking dread as she parked in the small Cameron Designs parking lot. And there was his white car, gleaming like he'd just washed it.

Why didn't you drive?

My car is white. I just washed it.

She hadn't spoken to him the rest of the weekend, which she now realized would make today awkward. It wasn't like they hung out after work...ever. But now that they'd seen each other naked, had shared his bed for a few hours early Saturday morning, things were going to be strained.

And she still couldn't explain what happened at the mansion. Terror on the high plains followed by the most amazing sex ever? Or... had it been okay sex masquerading as amazing? It'd been a while for her, and given the fact she'd been terrified, every sense, every nerve, every cell in her body was on high alert. Had that created a shroud of feelings that didn't really exist outside of being frightened out of her mind?

Hard to say, she thought, as she twisted her lips.

There was only one way to find out how things would go with him from here on out. She'd have to go inside and come face to face with him. She steeled herself and entered the building, but didn't see Marcus. She waved at the temp at the front desk and rounded the corner, running into Joanie on her way to her office.

"There you are!" She grinned, her hazel eyes shining, her dark, curly hair bobbing as she tilted her head. "Clive told me all about it. You know he wasn't supposed to be there that night, right? He wasn't supposed to slip out, and accompany Marcus on a stupid, childish mission to spook you out of your fair share of the bet." Her grin changed to concern, her eyebrows bending subtly. "You know I didn't know anything about it, right? Why didn't you call me this weekend? I just found out this morning, and it was filtered down from Marcus to Clive to me."

Lily shook her head at Joanie's machine gun chatter and gave her friend a nervous laugh. It was way too early, or Lily hadn't had enough coffee, or something... She had no idea how to answer any of Joanie's questions. She hadn't thought of Joanie at all until she was standing directly in front of her.

"Sounds like you're in the know," Lily said with a wan smile. Surely Marcus didn't tell Clive the one thing he promised not to. The sex thing. She'd kill him.

"Well, I guess the humiliation of getting scared out of the house by raccoons is salved by the fact that Marcus split the trip with you."

Split...the trip?

"I mean, I'm not going to lie." Joanie lowered her voice and took Lily's elbow. A minute later they were standing in Lily's darkened office. "The two of you together on this trip might be kind of awkward. Maybe you can just drink a lot of piña coladas and forget he's there."

"Good plan," Lily said, pretending she knew what was going on.

"Hawaii will be worth any discomfort. It's the least he owes you after sort of cheating to get it and sort of cheating to keep it." She laughed through the next words. "Clive told me about the mask, too. You should have kicked his ass!"

The mask. Raccoons. Clearly, Marcus had come in first thing this morning and worked some damage control. Lily did her best to play along.

"I should have," she agreed, a smile stuck to her face.

"Joanie!" Clive called, coming around the corner. "Oh, hey, Lil. Nicely done on snagging half the trip."

"Hi, Clive," she said flatly.

"Baxter on line three," he said to Joanie. "I have a conference call with Ed in two minutes. Can you take it?"

"Got it, babe," Joanie said, as Clive broke into a run down the hall. "Maxine Baxter is opening a new consignment shop. Wish me luck?"

Lily, head still spinning with uncertainty, flashed her friend a smile. "Luck."

Once Joanie walked away, Lily stood at the threshold of her office, blinking at her wall calendar. What just happened? She was five minutes late and this place was practically vibrating with energy. One thing was for sure—she needed to find out what Marcus had said to Clive…and what he hadn't.

Marcus's office was across the hall and down from hers. He was out of his chair, hovering over the drafting table, which meant he had hooked onto a really good idea. She'd seen him like that before. When he was working through something, he couldn't stay in his seat.

Maybe she shouldn't interrupt. Then again, how long could she play dumb? Since their offices were on one side of the building and Clive and Joanie's on the other, she didn't bother closing the door when she came in.

She tapped on the wall with her knuckles. "Hey."

Marcus lifted his head and turned to face her, his eyes hazy like he was still lost in thought.

"I can come back," she shot a thumb over her shoulder to point behind her. "Just wanted to return your mug." She placed the travel mug on his desk, her excuse for coming in there. Whispering, she added, "Didn't think I should bring your T-shirt into the office. It's in my car."

"Okay." He nodded, his expression unreadable. *Gosh. This is…weird.*

"Come here." Unlike the last time he'd said that to her—low and sexy, right before she punched a hole in the floor with her foot—his voice was gentle and inviting. She stepped deeper into his office, which was huge, with a desk on one side, a drafting table on the other, and a set of large file cabinets holding his drawings and current projects.

When she reached his side, he swiped bits of eraser off the wide sheet of paper on which he'd been drawing. "What do you think?"

"Main Street Salon," she read. A complete redesign. And it was gorgeous. Rather than being an open floor plan, now each sink and chair had its own partition—like a private room. "I like it."

"There will be a closet here for the customer to hang their coat and purse."

"It's great," she said, meaning it. "I'd get my hair done there."

"We all will. The owner offered us a deep discount." She glanced up at him and he winked. "She'll keep us pretty for years to come."

That smile again. She bit down on her lip, trying not to feel anything she shouldn't for him. But she couldn't help remembering the stubble against her nipples, the way his tongue felt gliding along her ear, the way he was demanding and sexy in the most perfect way…in the most unlikely place.

Say my name.

She cleared her throat and stole a peek behind her. Surely, Joanie and Clive were still on their calls. She kept her voice down anyway. "I ran into Joanie. She said she knew all about Friday."

He turned his back to the drafting desk, leaned against it, and crossed his thick arms. "Not all," he said.

"Care to tell me what parts?"

"I didn't tell him we…" His eyes flicked to the doorway then back to Lily. "You know."

Hearing him avoiding saying what they did would have been funny if she hadn't been so relieved. "Good."

His eyebrows drew together slightly.

"I assume you didn't tell them about the voices." She pursed her lips, then added, "The one you recorded or the ones we can't explain."

"Neither."

He turned back to his project. "It's not like anyone would believe us if we told them the truth."

The truth. About the voices, the footsteps… The other thing. The *them thing*.

"Raccoons seemed to be the easiest explanation," he said, palms on his desk as he studied the drawing in front of him. "Clive spilled the beans to Joanie about accompanying me to the house."

"And Joanie knew about the mask," Lily added.

"Traitor," he said. Then he flicked his eyes over at her and added a sheepish, "Sorry about that."

"Well. It's over now."

Something in his eyes darkened. She'd meant the night at Willow Mansion was over, but somehow it came out sounding like she meant the thing between them. And because that's where her head was, she wasn't sure what Marcus meant when he said in a wholly serious tone, "We'll see."

They shared a moment of silence. All she could hear was the soft hum of the copier running in the adjacent room. He stood away from his desk and rolled a pencil between his hands. "As far as the Hawaii thing, I meant it. If you don't mind sharing a trip with me, we'll split it. You can go as my plus one."

A long flight. A long vacation. A shared room. All with Marcus. She tried to make it sound bad in her head, but it didn't. It sounded fantastic.

"If you're not comfortable with that compromise," he said, "let me know and I'll find someone else to go with."

Jealousy spiked, sharp and angry. "Who?" she asked, the word coming out as barbed as the emotion pricking her.

He grinned, letting her know he'd set her up a little. "My brother would like to see the island."

Dammit. She needed to chill out. And make up her mind. Either they were doing the *them thing* or they weren't. Hawaii definitely sounded like a *them thing*.

"McIntire."

She tilted her chin to look up at him. His eyebrows were arched, the stubble around his mouth a tempting sight.

"Was just thinking on my feet," he said gently. "I wasn't trying to corner you."

"Yeah, no. Yes. It's… It totally makes sense. It's fine. And Hawaii is…fine."

A hint of his smile returned, like he was amused at her stammering. "Hawaii is fine."

"Totally fine." Her brittle smile broke at the edges and she backed away from him. "Well…"

"Well." He crossed his arms again, watching her closely.

Her forehead beaded with perspiration. Without saying another word, she turned and scuttled for her office across the hall. When she got there, she shut the door. She never shut the door, but right now, she needed to shut the door.

"Well," she said to herself as she plunked into her chair.

That was really all there was to say.

• • •

Marcus watched Lily's backside wiggle across the hall and into her office. Then he watched her shut her door and tried to remember the last time he looked across the hall and saw a panel instead of Lily's frown of concentration while she sat at her desk.

Never.

That, as they say, was that. He'd suspected she'd show up this morning and ignore him. Get right to work. If either of them was the consummate professional, it was Lily. In this case, he was glad to be wrong. Maybe her being willing to go to Hawaii with him meant she'd reconsidered about them.

Maybe not.

Women were hard.

He faced his drawing again, deciding distraction was the best medicine. He was pretty satisfied with what he'd come up with for the salon. Of course, he'd spent the remainder of the day Saturday and all of Sunday working on it, seeing how he didn't have a feisty, sexy redhead in his bed begging for sexual favors.

Shame.

The bright side to knuckling down all weekend, and coming in bright and early at five a.m. today was that he'd made a hell of a lot of progress. Nothing like pent-up frustration to fuel hours upon hours *upon hours* of work.

He should respect Lily for wanting to move forward and forget, and part of him did. The other part of him wanted to see what might come next. He'd never been so curious or intrigued by the next stage with a woman before. Even when he'd lived with Annie, the move-in had been a technicality. His lease was up, and her invitation was "You may as well."

With Lily, one night wasn't going to be enough to satisfy his curiosity—in bed or out. He wanted to explore whatever this was. Preferably before the RSD dinner. Them showing up with plus ones other than each other at this point would be...

Screw it. If it came to that, he'd go solo. He wasn't going to bring a nameless chick to the dinner and flaunt her in Lily's face. And he hoped she wouldn't call one of her exes just to avoid showing up alone.

So all he had to do was...he didn't know what. Killing every other guy she'd ever dated seemed extreme. Maybe he could tell her she had to be his date since she was getting half of Hawaii. He frowned. He wanted her to *want* to go with him. Why the hell did he want that? Getting her to comply wasn't enough. He wanted Lily willing. Ready *and* willing, he thought with a lift of his brows.

"Nice."

Marcus spun to find Clive stepping into his office, and he rerouted his thoughts away from Lily.

"Seriously," his friend said, approaching the drafting table. "Nice work."

Proudly, Marcus studied his drawings. "Thanks."

"I thought these weren't due until the fifth."

"They aren't. I had some time this weekend."

Clive grunted. "Didn't go like you wanted it to, I guess."

But it had. And it hadn't. Clive didn't wait for an answer, and Marcus was grateful.

"So, before the Retail Design Dinner, Joanie would like to have you and Lily over to the house to celebrate Reginald

London Superstores account."

"Didn't we do that at the Shot Spot?" The night he'd gotten to see Lily in a way he'd never seen her before. The night he'd made the bet that finally got her naked and underneath him.

"The Shot Spot, Joanie says, is not a proper celebration place."

Marcus figured she had a point. "Flat beer and stale pretzels, pool and a jukebox playing seventies country hits aren't her idea of a good time?"

Clive laughed. "Yeah. No. She is taking some French pastry class and wants to do dessert and champagne and set up the tables like some sort of patisserie." He shook his head and plunged his hands into his pockets. "I don't know. Anyway, you have to come."

"I do not." An intimate evening spent with Lily in front of the friends they weren't supposed to tell about their being together? Sounded like a disaster waiting to happen.

Marcus gestured at the drawings in front of him. "I'm pretty busy with this design."

"You're two weeks ahead of schedule."

"Then there's the speech," Marcus hedged. Not that he had to write it. It was written and rewritten. He'd cut it down, added to it, and finally arrived at something he thought he could get through without throwing up. That was the only goal at this point.

"Hey, you can't work all the time," Clive said, ignoring Marcus's excuses. "Sorry, buddy, not letting you back out of this one. "Friday night, seven."

"What if I have a date?" Marcus said in a last ditch effort to extricate himself.

"Lily's already invited." Clive grinned, a knowing look in his eyes.

Shit. His friend may not know what *exactly* happened at Willow mansion, but he knew too much already.

. . .

"There's no way. I'm...I'm so behind here," Lily threw her hands in the direction of her desk, which was covered with exactly three sheets of paper.

"Yeah," Joanie said, disbelief lining her voice. "You look *buried*." She folded her hands in front of her. "Please? I'm making croissants."

"I'm on a low-carb diet?" Lily offered, biting her lip.

Joanie sat in the chair across from Lily's desk. "The truth is," she whispered, "I'm inviting Reginald, too."

"Reginald London?" Just saying his name made her spine straighten.

Joanie nodded. "And his wife, Felicia. But don't tell Clive. I don't want him to be nervous."

"Why Marcus...I mean, why us? Why do *we* need to be there?" Just asking "why" made her sound as uncomfortable as she felt. Normally, she'd do whatever her friend asked.

"I need buffers! Those two are intimidating. Besides, you were the designers who won this account. I want to show you off." Joanie grinned.

Sweet, non-judgmental, clueless Joanie. How would Lily continue lying to her best friend? And who would she talk to about her confusing feelings if she couldn't confide in Joanie? And she couldn't. Joanie knew what happened with Emmett at Lily's former workplace. Surely, she'd have some advice to give. And she didn't think it'd be encouraging advice. Joanie was sweet and fun, but she was also smart and savvy. She owned this business, and her little firm had busted through a glass ceiling when Marcus won designer of the year. Lily wouldn't risk her own reputation, but she also wouldn't risk the reputation of her best friend's business. Not when she and Clive had worked so hard.

"Please? Just a few hours of munching on pastries and sipping champagne."

Lily sighed in defeat. "Can I bring anything?"

Joanie bounced up from the chair with a huge smile on her face. "Nope. Just yourself. Seven o'clock Friday, but if you want to show early you can watch me plate the food."

"Okay." Surely she and Marcus could coexist at a simple cocktail party.

"You're a doll!" Joanie blew her air kisses and exited the office.

Lily sagged in her chair and tried to think about what she'd wear. Marcus would prefer a short dress, and no panties. Which meant she should probably wear her stiff pantsuit and chunky jewelry.

An email notification slid onto the corner of her computer screen. Normally, she would have checked it later, but she could have sworn the name that popped up had said...

A few quick clicks had her stomach sinking like a stone surrounded by concrete.

Emmett Webster.

The very man who had claimed she'd stolen his design to get ahead. The man who wooed her and promised no one would find out about the office fling, then advertised it after knowing their sexist pig of a boss would take Emmett's word over hers.

The loss of the job had been upsetting to say the least, but the loss of her hard work and reputation, having to rebuild completely, had been devastating.

And now, two years later, out of the blue, he was emailing her?

Don't open it.

But she would. Of course she would.

"Hey Lily of the Valley!" the email started. Lily because of her name, Valley because of her cleavage. Stupidest nickname ever, and he thought he was being just *so* clever. He did it to irritate her. Mission accomplished. Everything about him irritated her. She steeled herself and read the rest.

Hey Lily of the Valley!

I heard through the grapevine, namely Reginald London who I now work for, that you were over at Cameron Designs. You're probably stoked to be in a small office with friends without the pressure you were under before.

The dig didn't escape her attention—his way of saying she couldn't make it in a big corporate office. The bastard. And why would London hire him? Did she owe the universe a major debt or something?

Anyway, just wanted to drop you a line and let you know I'd see you at the RSD dinner this year. I skipped the last two, just wasn't into it.

Why this year, then? Just to ruin her life?

I've been asked to present the designer of the year award and wanted to give you a heads up since it's a guy from your office. Marcus Black. He's damned impressive. The design for London's store is fantastic and we can't stop talking about him over here. Just remember not to wear anything too revealing

*to the dinner. You don't want everyone to assume you have
more boobs than brains! LOL.*

See you, babe.

Emmett

Lily didn't know what to be more offended by: the "more
boobs than brains" thing or the "babe" thing. The insult was
something she'd heard often from him when they dated. The
fact that he'd gone out of his way to bring it up now proved
his habit of marginalizing her—controlling her—was alive
and well.

Marcus had added the short-skirt-no-panties thing into
the bet for the RSD dinner, and she'd shrugged it off as boys
being boys. But weighed against Emmett's shit-for-brains
email, Marcus's dare sort of proved that he respected her
at work. He didn't worry someone would get the wrong im-
pression just because she dressed sexy. He knew she had
brains and boobs and respected both parts of her. She knew
because at Willow Mansion he'd told her just how big a part
she'd played in landing the London account. She didn't think
he was just saying that, no more than she was when she told
him he was the best in the business. That was a rare revealing
moment between them…followed by an even more revealing moment.

Anyway.

Focus.

She tore her mind off Marcus's delicious abs and bare
chest and glared at the word "babe" in the signoff on Emmett's email. The moniker "asshat" she'd teasingly assigned
to Marcus belonged firmly after Emmett D. Webster's name.

Maybe she'd just show Emmett and wear not only a
short skirt to the dinner, but also a low-cut top, high heels,

and zero undergarments. An evil smile stole over her face.

Yes. Maybe she'd do that. Then her smile vanished. She couldn't let Emmett—or anyone—know that she was there with Marcus, though. Not if she didn't want her past making an unwanted comeback...like acid-washed jeans.

"McIntire." Marcus stepped into her office and lifted a takeout menu. "Chinese?"

On the heels of that email, his presence was a breath of fresh, musky, pine-scented air. "Sure."

"Let me guess." He put the menu to his forehead, closed his eyes, and pretended to read her mind. "Kung Pao chicken, spice level number seven."

Damn. Exactly right. She crossed her arms over her breasts. "Okay, smarty. Like you're *not* going to order the orange beef, level ten, with a double order of crab rangoon?"

"Level *twelve*." He pointed the menu like he had something on her.

"That sounds hot," she said, a smile curving her lips.

"Honey, you have no idea." With a wink, he turned and held up the menu as Clive passed him in the hallway. "Chinese?" she heard him ask.

Face warm from Marcus's departing comment, Lily deleted Emmett's email with a decisive *click*.

Chapter Fourteen

The rest of the week went as per their usual.

Sort of.

Lily ran into Marcus in the morning scarfing down donuts near the coffeemaker. They ate lunch in the conference room together everyday, and discussed projects. But what wasn't normal was how there were at least two times when she would have gone to his office to ask his opinion, but she hadn't. She'd gone to Joanie instead, and Clive once, too. Avoidance wasn't like her, and it wasn't like Marcus to let her get away with it.

She supposed they were both being careful. Which should have made her feel better but the circumventing was...silly. It made the get-together at Clive and Joanie's house tomorrow night seem all the more challenging since she and Marcus hadn't really talked things through yet.

"How many of these do you think I can fit into my mouth at once?"

She looked up from her design for the end caps for a local pet shop, which she updated once a month, to see Marcus with a jar of gumballs in his hand. "Why...would you do that?"

He shrugged. "You like to dare me to do things."

"No, *you* like to dare *me* to do things. I like to work."

He abandoned the gumballs on the corner of her desk. "Gift from Lonnie over at the candy store for the design we did last month."

"Oh, thoughtful."

"Are we going to talk about what happened at the mansion?"

She looked away from the colorful gumballs. Marcus had his feet crossed at the ankles and was leaning in her doorway, arms crossed, muscles standing out in his forearms. She pictured him without a shirt and got lightheaded.

"The ghost?" she asked.

"The sex," he said. Bluntly.

Her cheeks grew warm and then warmer when he straightened, closed the door, and crossed the room. He sat on the corner of her desk, one khaki-encased thigh really close to her. She allowed her eyes to move up to his face. "Okay."

"You don't want to have sex with me again," he stated.

So not true.

"I... don't think we should," she said, then volleyed back, "Do you?"

"You think the mansion was a fluke."

He wasn't going to answer her questions either, she could see. "I think it was...intense there. The environment. The circumstance."

"Intense."

Flashes of what happened lit the screen of her memory and her breasts grew heavy. Her face was downright hot. Marcus tipped her chin with one finger. "I dare you to go back for one more night with me."

She nearly choked. "Are you insane?"

"No, determined. To prove to you what's between us wasn't a trick of the light. We have something that could be something, McIntire. But I need you to admit it."

Shuffling papers that didn't need shuffling was a great way to avoid looking at him. "Well, I'm…that's not going to happen. Willow Mansion can keep all my things because I'm not setting foot back in that haunted funhouse."

"Or back in bed with me."

She shook her head, chickening out. The truth was she'd love to, but it was also true that there was too much on the line if she did.

He nodded in response, but it was robotic. Grim. When he opened her door, she stopped him with, "Your jar."

"Keep them," he said. "We'll see if you're able to keep your hands off me tomorrow night."

He shut her door behind him and she stared at the pink, blue, white, yellow, and orange gumballs in the jar. He'd just issued a dare of another kind, and against her better sense the challenge sounded just as sweet as the multi-colored candies staring back at her.

• • •

Joanie had said "nothing fancy." *Hmph*.

Lily scanned her closet, scraping hangers left then right,

then right then left again. Nothing. She had nothing to wear save for her standard work wardrobe. And why did she care? Certainly not because Marcus would be there. Certainly not because she would be seeing him during the cover of night for the first time since the mansion. Certainly not because he'd dropped as juvenile (and sweat-inducing) a challenge as "bet you can't keep your hands off me."

Good lord, he wasn't *that* irresistible.

Was he?

Anyway, it wasn't like she would morph into a sex-crazed monster at the sight of the full moon. She let loose a laugh, but it was an uneasy one. She couldn't just…have sex with him again. She pulled a delicate, slightly see-through blouse out of her closet and frowned. Could she?

Not without a really good reason.

How about because he makes you see stars when he kisses you?

Yeah, that. Not to mention that watching his shoulders move under his clothes while they were at work had soaked her brain in memories of him shirtless, sliding into her, saying her name…

Oh, Lord. She put the blouse back into her closet and traded it for a less-sheer shirt.

Tonight was such a bad idea.

Lily and Clive's 1900s home stood on the edge of a sidewalk, old and brick, structurally beautiful. A cherry tree dominated their miniscule front lawn, and a short wrought iron fence looped their property, including the quaint backyard filled with more trees.

As she stepped over the leaves littering the walk, she heard a car pull up to the curb. Nerves jumped like jackrabbits in her stomach. It was six o'clock, but dusk had fallen, giving the neighborhood a spooky fall feeling.

A car door closed. Heavy shoes approached from behind her, crunching leaves beneath their soles. She scaled the porch steps, still not turning, picturing the man embodying those sounds: the wide frame, the girth and length that had settled between her thighs a few days ago, the way his tongue swept her nipples, the rogue glint in his eyes as he admired her nakedness.

Okay, she'd become a little sex obsessed since he'd made her say his name. Sue her.

At the door, she turned, flipped her hair off her shoulder, and locked eyes with Marcus. He was climbing the stairs, wearing a pair of black dress pants and a gray dress shirt. His hair was damp as if he'd just showered, and he smelled… wow. Heavenly. Like fall itself had cloaked him.

"You look hot," he said, the side of his mouth hitching.

She shook her head and smiled, ran a hand down her simple black skirt. "You have a way with words."

"I speak the truth." He tipped his head toward the door. "You knock yet?"

She shook her head.

"We're early."

"We are."

They stood in silence for a moment.

"Walk with me."

She pulled a breath into her lungs and turned away from the door. Dinner didn't start for an hour.

Taking her silence for acquiescence, he took her hand and pulled her down the steps. The pace casual, they started down the sidewalk as a gentle, cool breeze blew. His fingers laced with hers.

"Talk to me, McIntire," he said when they'd gotten a few houses away from the Camerons'.

"Um." She thought for a second then asked, "How's the speech going?"

He slid her a look. "Talk to me about something else."

She grinned up at him. "Still nervous about that?"

"Know what I'm nervous about?"

Her heart mule-kicked her chest. Her? Them? Getting her to admit that she missed him more now that they'd slept together? It was as if she hadn't known what she was missing, and now she did.

Also, she was afraid he would win that bet he'd made yesterday. Technically, she thought as she looked down at their linked fingers, he already had. She couldn't keep her hands off him.

"Tonight," he said.

Well. There was no better intro than that. She dropped his hand and walked to the corner. He followed. When they reached the stop sign, she opened her mouth, and then closed it while she waited for a woman walking her dog to pass.

"It's something, isn't it? This…what's between us?" she asked. It wasn't smart. It wasn't what she should want, but in the dead of night, in the bright morning, in the days since the mansion where she tried, and failed, to forget what happened between them, she'd realized there was no denying a spark had ignited. And if she couldn't deny it, she needed to deal with it.

He didn't laugh her off, change the subject, or shy away. "Yes."

"At first I thought maybe it was the mansion. Because we were afraid. Adrenaline was up…or something."

"Or something." His dark eyes heated. He took a step closer to her and grasped her hips, his nostrils flaring as he took slow inventory of every inch of her face.

"Looks like you're the one who can't keep your hands off me," she said, her heart thundering in her eardrums.

"Looks like." He kissed her, slow and soft at first, then harder as he slid his tongue into her mouth. Her palm went to the back of his head, and her body molded into his. Nipples erect, she rubbed against him, wanting…gosh. Just wanting him so much it hurt. She'd thought about him all week: in the shower this morning, in her bed, at lunch…

But what she wanted most of all was him inside her.

He tore his mouth from hers, sucking in a breath and twining his fingers in her hair. "Come home with me, McIntire."

"I…we have the party." But a certain spot between her legs throbbed the word *yes* in Morse code.

"After the party." His eyes grew dark, his tone dropped even lower. "Let me take you to my bed," he said, moving his hands from her hair and running his fingertips down her neck. She suppressed a shudder. "And I'll show you all the ways you can come beneath me." His grip tightened on her hips. "And on top of me."

She tried to find her voice. Impossible.

He smirked, knowing he was getting to her, that her resolve was eroding the more he talked. "And in front of me, Lily."

"Okay" was on the tip of her tongue, but she couldn't say it.

Apparently he didn't need to hear it, or had read the answer in her eyes, because next he took her hand and walked toward Joanie and Clive's house once again.

"It's just cocktails and dessert," he said. "How long could it last?"

• • •

An eternity.

Cocktails and dessert could last until the dawn of a new fucking age.

Marcus smiled tightly at Reginald, who'd been blathering on about…God. He had no clue. He'd tuned him out eons ago.

He slipped a look over his shoulder at Lily, who was standing, wineglass in hand, poised with a smile on her face he'd bet was as strained as the one on his. Oh, if Felicia London, who was talking with her hands and flashing what looked like several hundred karats of diamond jewelry, knew what was under that polite façade. Joanie, who stood in that little circle, caught Marcus's eyes and rolled hers. Yeah, drinks and dessert had gone a little longer than she'd planned, as well.

Clive had managed to avoid Marcus and Reginald both. Because he was smart. And a dick. He knew if he got roped into Reginald's storytelling he'd be rooted to the same spot for ages. Well. Marcus had been rooted on this same spot and was in desperate need of a break. When Clive walked by on his way to the bar to refill his wine, Marcus tuned into the tail end of what Reginald was saying.

"...and mounted it in my den. Big moose." Reginald nodded and pushed his glasses up on his nose. "Big-ass moose, Marcus."

"You know, Clive was telling me a hunting story the other day," Marcus said. Clive, hearing his name, turned his head, then narrowed his eyelids. Marcus grinned and continued lying his pants off. "You remember, Clive. The one about the deer. And the rabbits." He turned to Reginald. "Hilarious. Wait'll you hear it." He backed a few steps away when Reginald turned his attention to Clive. "If you'll excuse me for a minute, I have to visit the facilities."

He swaggered away, but not before hearing Clive start a story that did not until just now exist. He caught Lily's eye as he went. She lifted one prim eyebrow. He winked. Joanie and Felicia were ensconced in conversation, and as he walked past in the direction of the bathroom, he heard Lily excuse herself as well.

Clive and Joanie's house was big, and given the fact he'd been there about nine hundred and forty-three times, Marcus knew his way around. The huge eat-in kitchen contained a dining room table that sat ten, a breakfast bar and island in the center of the room, and a newly built pantry Clive and Marcus had designed a few months back. The pantry not only stocked food but also had a humidor for cigars and shelving to hold bottles of wine.

It was kick-ass. He'd just stopped in front of its double doors when he heard heels click behind him. He turned and snagged Lily's arm, opened the pantry, and closed them inside.

He had her up against a wall in a nanosecond, his mouth

fused with hers a second later. She tasted like crisp white wine, apples, and something else… Her, he realized. It was a taste he'd gotten a sample of at the end of the block, a taste he hadn't been able to forget since the night at Willow Mansion. Much as he wanted to make an excuse and leave, he hadn't found an opening yet. And this, *her*, was exactly what he needed. Her palms went to his chest, her touch burning him down to the soles of his dress shoes.

After parting, she breathed, "I'm about to fake a burst appendix."

"Joanie would insist on coming to the hospital," he reminded her, his hands sliding down her lower back and over her skirt.

"I know. What about you, can you fake something?"

"Not me, baby. I'm a hundred percent real."

A grin took over her lips, and then she shocked the hell out of him by cupping his junk in one hand. His semi- was becoming a full-on. And fast.

"Yep," she purred up at him. "That's real, all right."

She unbuttoned his slacks. "I figure since we can't ignore what's between us, we'll just have to indulge."

"How much have you had to drink?" he couldn't help but ask. It wasn't like her to be careless, or risky.

"It's been a long week, Black." She unzipped him next, reaching into his underwear and squeezing his cock. He grunted and she shushed him. "Anyway, stop talking."

He swallowed and dutifully kept his mouth shut, his blood roaring as Lily stroked him again. She backed him into a shelf, sending boxes of cereal wobbling behind him. His senses were heightened in the dark. It was like they were back in the mansion, groping in the dark and finding each other. Lily's hands tugged his pants and boxers down, and she slid to her knees in front of him. A sliver of light from the crack under the door allowed him a tease of what she had planned. And he liked what he saw.

From the champagne, or maybe the rush of lust, Lily's inhibitions were down, her guard dropped, and Marcus would have been all for it—okay, *was* all for it—but for the fact that their best friends were a few rooms over with their latest clients...

God. This was stupid. Was he really going to let Lily go down on him while—

He felt the tip of her tongue flick over his cock and he conked his skull against some cans behind him.

Yes. Hell yes, he was.

"Kiss me, beautiful," he begged, wanting those lips again.

"Oh, I plan on it." She smiled against his skin, then wrapped her lips around the head of his penis.

Aaaaaand...he was going to die.

He'd always thought of blowjobs as gifts from above, especially when an exquisite creature was willing and ready to perform one. He didn't like to brag, but he'd gotten more than a few girls on their knees. He thought he knew just what to expect.

Except he hadn't counted on Lily.

Once she licked the head, she scraped the fleshy part with her teeth, then sucked, then repeated the process. The sensations shooting up his spine were nothing short of glorious. He gripped the shelf behind him with one hand and wound the fingers of his other hand into her hair while she worked. And damn, she was working it. Working him. He thought she'd continue worshipping the tip, which, hey, he had zero problems with, but then her mouth opened and she swallowed him down, taking in every inch while he sucked a breath through his teeth and tried to maintain. What he wanted to do was pull her mouth off his cock, ruck that skirt up over her hips, and plunge deep inside her.

But since they were on borrowed minutes before Clive or Joanie or, God help him, both of them, came looking, he guessed he wouldn't get that far.

Damn shame, too. Not that he wasn't enjoying her mouth on him. A little too much, actually.

"McIntire," he grunted, fisting her hair in his hand as she hummed, taking him deeper. The sound reverberated in his balls and tingled low in his spine.

"Lily, I—oh, fuck." Whatever words he'd been planning to say shot out of his brain like a cannonball. He dropped his head against the shelf, bonking his head again and not caring even a little. He loosened his grip on her hair, enjoying the feel of her soft lips, lapping tongue, and the added bonus of her hand wrapped around the base of his shaft.

Then she picked up the pace. Yep. He was going to lose it.

Close. So, *so* close. Her fingers wrapped him tighter and he thrust his hips, sending him deeper into her mouth. She didn't mind, either, opening wide to accommodate him. On the edge of coming, he was snapped back by an incredibly unwelcome interruption.

"Tawny port. We picked it up when we were in California last year," came Joanie's muffled voice growing ever closer to the pantry.

He lost Lily's mouth in an instant. She rose to her feet and he jerked his pants over his hips and his cock while

Joanie's voice grew nearer, talking about notes of vanilla and how "one glass will do ya!"

Meanwhile, Marcus tucked his shirt in, bumping the head of his erection and wincing at the pain. He was right. He *was* going to die, but not in the fun way like he'd imagined earlier.

"Decent?" Lily whispered.

"Hardly," he grunted.

The handle on the door turned and Marcus tugged Lily out of the way and hit the switch on the wall, bathing them in light. Her hair was disheveled, her lips plump, and his dick gave another mournful bob.

"Oh!" Joanie pressed a hand to her chest and Felicia stood next to her, looking equally shocked.

"Found it!" Lily shouted, reaching for a can behind Marcus's head. She held up a can of cherry pie filling and Marcus wanted to howl. Good luck explaining that one. "Sorry. Can I borrow this?" She stepped in front of him, helpfully shielding his pants from view. "Oh, wait. Never mind." She shook her head and replaced the can. "I thought that was peach."

Joanie's eyebrows rose significantly higher. "What…are you doing?"

"Marcus was showing me the newly redesigned pantry—looks great, by the way—and then he thought he'd be cute and shut the door on me," Lily said. "He knows how afraid of the dark I am."

Oh, boy. She was terrible at making things up on the fly.

"And then after letting me freak out for a minute, I got ahold of the switch. Thank goodness, because after the night at Willow—"

"Never gonna let her live that down," he interrupted

with what he hoped was an easy smile.

"That's a story…" Joanie started.

"For another day," Lily said. "I'm so, so sorry, but I have to get going. I'm just…exhausted."

"I was just going to open a bottle of port. Care for a glass?" Joanie asked.

"No," they answered at the same time.

"We'll, uh… We'll get out of your way." Marcus steered Lily in front of him and out of the pantry.

"Yeah." Oh, hell. Joanie knew something was up. And unless Felicia was stone deaf and blind to boot, so did she. Joanie covered smoothly, showing off the pantry and the wine shelves as Felicia commented on the vintages. But as Marcus navigated Lily through the kitchen, they encountered Clive and Reginald close behind him.

"Hey, guys," Clive said, the words strung out into a series of long vowels. "What's up?"

"Clive was telling me what a great poker player you are, Mr. Black," Reginald said, evidently clueless as to why Lily's hair was crushed and Marcus looked like a deer in headlights. "Cigars and poker."

"Can't." Marcus kept Lily in front of him so as not to expose what was really between them. *All eight-and-a-half inches of it.* "Just got a text from my brother. He needs a lift. Car broke down."

"Well, we—er, I should go, too," Lily said. "My fish needs food and…" She didn't even finish her sentence. Clive looked bemused.

Marcus clasped onto Lily's hips like they were doing the conga and chased her out of the room. "See you Monday, Clive. Enjoy the poker game, Reginald. Another time, I'll go all in." Another time when he wasn't so close to going all in with Lily.

"Drive safe, you two," Clive called after him.

Out in the dining room, Lily beelined for the closet and tore her coat off a hanger, then slung her purse over one shoulder. "See you at my place," she said as he opened the door.

"Your place?" Marcus felt his eyebrows lift.

She grinned as she slipped past him. "Mine's closer."

Chapter Fifteen

So, this wasn't like her. Usually.

She'd tried to be practical, tried to resist him. As she'd watched Marcus from across the room, Lily decided, *To hell with it.*

She wasn't drunk, but the champagne she'd sipped had made her feel loose and carefree, and the idea of stealing a kiss from Marcus to tide her over—if they ever got to leave the Camerons' house—had cemented in her mind.

Then in the dark of the pantry, things had gotten a little out of hand. It was the dark. The perceived danger, the adrenaline spike…

It was Willow Mansion. Only without the cockroaches and smashing sounds.

She flicked a glance at her rearview mirror. It wasn't just the mansion, but the man following behind her. Something about Marcus sent her brain packing. *Clearly*, since she'd taken him into her mouth in the pantry of her best friend's house.

"God. I'm a hussy," she said to herself.

Unfortunately, or fortunately—too soon to tell—she didn't have any more time to think, since she only lived seven minutes from Joanie and Clive's house. Marcus pulled his sparkling white car to the curb behind hers.

Lily. Finally. Out of my dreams.

She watched him get out, took in his easy swagger as he approached her car. Something told her she'd gotten in way too deep way too fast.

"If you think I followed you here," he said as she swung her car door open, "to get you to finish what you started..."

"Marcus," she hissed. Her neighbors were too elderly to hear much, but still.

"You're right." He grinned and her eyes went to the dimple denting his face.

He was so hot.

"Eventually. I have plans for you first," he said, taking her hand and lacing their fingers. Such an intimate move without being intimate. It was something she'd done with her boyfriends since junior high. So why, when Marcus took her hand, did she melt into his side?

Because he's warm and big and strong... And because she liked him way too much.

"Why do I think you're turning something over in your head you aren't sharing?"

Because I am.

"Joanie and Clive..."

"We'll smooth it over," he said.

She let him end the conversation. She didn't want to talk or think about it. She wedged the key into her door. Her townhouse was a double, two-story brick and old like the house they'd just come from, with a red-orange brick porch and square concrete pillars holding the overhang. Her right-next-door neighbor, Phyllis, had been in bed since eight o'clock, no doubt, but her large, scrappy yellow tomcat, Harvey, leaped to the dividing wall between their porches and let out a sickly *Meower!*

"Good Lord," Marcus said, hitching an eyebrow.

"Harvey, meet Marcus. Marcus, my neighbor's cat, Harvey."

"*Meower!*"

"Is he...sick?" He scratched the cat's head and Harvey leaned into his palm and made the sickly noise again, followed by a sputtering purr.

"He's not. He just has a speech impediment."

She pushed her front door open, aware of Marcus following her inside, very closely, then shutting the door behind him. "Well, this is my place."

But any nickel tour or offer of a nightcap was cut off when he turned her with his hands and laid his lips on hers. And oh, he tasted good. He'd tasted good *down there*, too, all manly and clean, and his tongue tasted...wow. Incredible.

He explored her mouth as he slipped her purse off her shoulder and dropped it on the floor. She reached out and tossed her keys onto the entertainment stand, which held a modest television, a fish bowl—where she saw Bubbles flicking around animatedly—and her stereo system.

"One second." She tore her mouth from Marcus's, tapped a few flakes into the bowl, and then came back to her date, looping her arms around his neck.

"You really have a fish," he said, running those wide

palms down over her shoulders and ribs, and then back up, where he swept them over her breasts. "I thought you were just saying that."

"Nope. I am with fish."

He lit her up with another kiss, squeezing her breasts gently and then lowering his palms to her backside and squeezing there, too. His eyes were closed, those long, dark lashes brushing the tops of his cheeks. Stubble scraped her sensitive skin as he slanted his mouth and deepened their kiss. She allowed her eyes to sink closed, too, gradually losing sense of time and space, and the ability to stand. When her knees went gooey, and she moaned against his lips, she felt him smile.

"Bedroom," he said, low and growly.

"Upstairs." Her voice was not growly. It was breathy and quiet and sounded more like a wheeze. What had this man done to her?

He took her hand again and dragged—yes, dragged—her up the stairs, his long legs taking two at a time while she raced to keep up. The closer they drew to her room, the heavier her feet became. He pointed at one of the two bedroom doors, both closed. "This one?"

"That one," she said, pointing to the end of the hall.

His eyebrows lowered. "You okay?"

She nodded. "I guess. Just…a little nervous."

"Don't be." He hugged her close, kissing her as he subtly moved closer to her bedroom. "We've done this before."

She smiled. They had. "We were pretty good at it…I think. Unless it was just the mansion."

"Told you we could go back, and I'd prove to you it wasn't just the mansion." He popped open her door. "Though

I think we can prove it just as well in here."

He lowered his lips to hers, his fingers gripping the tab of the plastic zipper at the back of her skirt, sliding it down and reaching beneath the material. "Lace," he commented, squeezing her butt. "Tell me they're red."

She smiled against his mouth, fear receding into something much more welcome: lust. "They're black."

"Acceptable," he murmured against her mouth, before kissing her deeply again.

His hands went to her blouse next, those big fingers clumsily working the delicate pearl buttons. He fumbled through a few before he said, "I'll buy you a new one," then tore the shirt open.

Since she had carpet, there was no rolling of buttons to be heard. Pity. Marcus had just fulfilled a fantasy of hers. She'd always wanted someone to rip her shirt off.

He cupped her breasts and smashed them together, burying his face in her cleavage. Then he licked between them before darting along the edge of her bra. He grazed a nipple and her hands moved to his head, her fingers crushing his hair. He didn't seem to mind, repeating the move on the other breast while she squirmed. Her hips wiggled urgently.

"Impatient." But he didn't torture her further, fisting the sides of her skirt and yanking it down. A guttural sound of appreciation echoed in his throat before he pressed his face against her lace panties and tugged with his teeth. Then those were gone, too, snatched away and sliding south. Her bedroom lamp was on—she always left it on as a safety precaution when she was out after dark—so she could see everything he was doing.

And what he was doing was...staring. Watching the apex

of her thighs while untangling the scrap of material from her ankles. He slipped her shoes away as well, getting her good and naked, save for the bra still hiding her breasts.

From his knees he looked up at her, dark brown eyes filled with a hazy brand of passion that made her shiver all over. "You're bare."

She was.

The first time he'd undressed her she'd made an excuse for not being prepared for "company" and while he'd had no problem with the triangle of smooth, reddish curls he'd found, Lily wanted to surprise him in case there was a next time. "Do you like it?"

"More than like, sweetheart." Roughened palms slid up her thighs and over her hips. He parted her, lowered his face, and slicked his tongue along her center.

Oh. Oh, yes. Yes, yes, yes.

"Way more than like," he mumbled against her.

Her head dropped back on her neck. How long had it been since she'd had a man's face between her thighs? Too long. Too, too long. And really, it was because she didn't let just anyone down there. This took a lot of trust and—

"*Marcus.*" Her hands were in his hair, guiding his head back and forth as his tongue assaulted her. She lost his mouth, and a petulant grunt came from her next. Finally, she let a guy down there, and he had no desire to stay. Bummer.

But she'd misread him, clearly, because then he said, "On the bed. What I have planned for you will render you unable to stand."

Her eyebrows lifted as he rose to his full height over her. "What...what do you have planned?"

"About an hour of that. I'm good at it." He ducked his

head and kissed her lips, and she tasted herself on his mouth.

She'd just bet.

"I'll have you writhing," he said, tugging her nipples. "Soaked." He tugged again and licked his tongue over her lips. "Begging me to stop."

"Wanna bet?" she breathed, trying to joke to find her footing in this moment.

"You'll lose."

She grinned. "And win."

"We'll all win." He slapped her ass, just a quick sting of a touch, and pointed to her bed.

Her nipples hardened when she thought of what was coming soon to a bedspread near her, and Lily crawled onto the bed and lay flat on her back.

. . .

Marcus wasn't lying when he said he was good at this.

He knew what women liked, and even though he and Lily had been together one time—if he didn't count the pantry—he was pretty sure he knew what *she* liked.

He unbuttoned his shirt, flattered when she watched hungrily as he bared his chest to her. He felt the small smile inching across his mouth but buried it, not wanting to take her out of the moment. Still. Her attention made him puff with male pride.

He shed his pants, shoes, and socks, leaving his boxer briefs, slightly damp from her exploration earlier.

"I didn't get to finish what I started in the pantry," she said quietly.

His dick jerked to attention. *Down, boy.*

"Would you like to?" he asked.

"Yes, please." She nodded eagerly.

Damn. He liked that.

"We'll arrange for that. But first…" He put his knee on the bed and dipped his chin. "Spread your legs."

She smiled, the fire in her eyes matching the strawberry in her hair. Obediently, she spread her legs.

"Beautiful." His voice was a comical mixture of rumbling and reverent. Eyes glued to the recently bared part of her, he made room between her thighs with his shoulders. Parting her folds, he held her open and slicked his tongue along her slowly.

She bucked against his face.

Sensitive, too. Oh, this was going to be fun.

He glanced up at her, licking her again. She had thrown her hands out and fisted the sheets. So he continued. And was rewarded for his efforts by a thrusting, moaning woman whose cheeks and chest flushed when she came.

And came again.

"Please, Marcus," she panted, clamping her thighs over his ears. He pulled her legs apart and increased the pressure against her clit. "I can't." Her protest was a shout as she tried unsuccessfully to squirm away. "Please! No more, no… oh! Oh! Marcus!"

He didn't let up, holding her legs and feeling her pulse against his tongue. Her screaming faded into mewls which faded into what sounded like a soft sob. And this time she'd said his name without any prompting at all. It was a great gift.

He let her go, her legs falling open as he leaned over her at the top of the bed. He lifted the very limp arm she'd thrown over her face and dropped it to the side. He smoothed her hair—gone curly, since her temples were damp with sweat—away from her forehead.

"Told you you'd beg," he reminded her.

"Hmm," she hummed, satisfied. He could see the *satisfied*. Her eyes opened lazily, blinking even more lazily. "Wow."

His grin was genuine. And yes, cocky. He couldn't help it. Seeing her this pleased, he felt like he'd won some sort of kinky lottery.

One of her hands slipped over his boxer briefs and squeezed. He was hard, getting harder now that she was touching him. "I'm doing you next."

"No. You're not." He dipped his head in reference to the part of her he was just enjoying. "I want in there."

A laugh sounded in her throat, also making him feel proud. "You have a way with words, Black."

"I have a way with you, McIntire." He lowered over her, kissing her, running his tongue along the tip of hers. "You are powerless beneath me."

Her eyes flared with heat, this time directed at him, and not what he was doing to her. He wanted that—wanted her seeing him as he was, not who she'd mistakenly assumed him to be. He may have been playing the field for a while, but if Lily was game, she was the only field he had any interest in. The realization scared the hell out of him, but there it was.

"Condom," she said.

"Like it when you're impatient." He left her briefly to fish a foil packet out of his pants pocket. He may have happened to buy a box and tuck it under the passenger seat of his car. And he may have torn off three of them and stuffed them into his pocket when he pulled up behind her at her house.

He rolled off his boxers and rolled on the condom before climbing up her sweet body, positioning himself, and sinking deep. Throwing her head back, she screamed again. Loud.

"God, you're sensitive," he told her.

She moaned.

He thrust his hips forward, going deeper, and was rewarded with another moan, accompanied by her fingernails clawing down his back. He continued pumping into her as she held on, legs wide, arms tightening around his back, and soon she was coming again, her inner muscles clamping down on him and causing him to wedge his teeth together.

Clasping his face between her palms, she watched him, eyes open, lips parted, expelling breath after breath of ecstasy.

"You," she said. "You." Before he became flattered, she looked almost angry when she growled, "Come. I'm dying."

He was buried in her to the hilt, and he'd been moving at a fast clip, but he could feel her pulsing.

Her anger faded from her face, and again she requested, "Please."

He uttered a small laugh and kissed her lips. "Okay, but only because you asked nice." Then he started again, torturing her—and himself. A few minutes in, and damned if she didn't go off again, milking his orgasm from him.

After a few more involuntary thrusts, he collapsed on top of her, smashing her into the covers with half his body. He was still inside her, balls pounding, head swimming, as her hands stroked his back.

"Black," she whispered, kissing his face.

"Mmm," he said, eyes still shut.

"Thank you." She sounded so grateful, he couldn't stop

himself.

He laughed.

• • •

Marcus's wide shoulders shook and Lily felt her smile widen.

Had she ever had this much fun in bed? Then she thought of the half-dozen orgasms she'd had under this man's ministrations and decided that *no*, she had not ever, ever had this much fun in bed.

Refreshing, really. He looked refreshed, too. She liked that she'd made him feel as good as she did.

"You always this responsive?" he asked, jolting her out of her bliss.

"Meaning?" she asked.

His hand found her breast. "Meaning, are you always this easy to please?"

She slapped his arm halfheartedly. He chuckled again.

"I'm not answering that question," she said. "You just want to know if I'm reacting this way only with you."

Something serious crossed his face as his thumb stroked over her nipple. "Was it me?"

Yes.

She didn't say it, but she didn't have to. He grinned and nuzzled her nose with his. "Yeah. It was me."

"You know, you do not have ego problems."

"I have another problem." He shifted his hips. "Don't want to leave."

She froze, wondering if he meant her body or her bed.

A second later, he disconnected from her so slowly, he took her next breath with him.

"Damn," he said, pegging her with a sexy smile. Then he was up, standing at the side of her bed. "I assume your bathroom is at the end of the hall."

"The room with the toilet in it," she called as he walked away from her. She watched his athletic butt and bit her lip.

"Ha-ha," came his response, just before the door shut behind him.

Now what?

Should she ask him to stay? True, she'd slept over at his house last weekend, but then, she'd been thoroughly exhausted from an evening of spent adrenaline. She sensed tonight would be different. There wasn't anything otherworldly between them. And maybe that was the problem. There was no distraction here in her safe, quiet little townhome, and that meant if she asked him to stay and he did...they'd be bare.

She tugged the sheet over her body, thinking they'd been pretty bare all-around a few minutes ago. Why did she care? She'd like to spin herself a tale of her ex and the way she'd been betrayed, but she and Marcus were beyond that, and she knew it. Plus, after they'd tumbled out of the Cameron pantry looking so guilty, she was pretty sure her friends could guess what was up. That left the only other reason she didn't want Marcus to stay.

Because she was scared to try again and get burned. Especially to go all in with a guy she worked with, because if they broke up and she still had to see him forty hours a week, that would be...ugly.

Unless... things worked out?

That thought sent a blaze of hope into her bloodstream, made her fast forward her future and see the epic possibilities of family, of children, of…everything. And she didn't want everything. She couldn't handle everything. She could handle the sex. She could even handle fudging their story for the sake of keeping Joanie and Clive's reputation on level. But she wasn't sure she could handle commitment after her last commitment ended so very badly.

Still. It'd be nice to have him here. Maybe for another round of sex. Some snacks and television. A shower.

A smile curved her lips as Marcus, bare-assed naked, and ridiculously gorgeous, swaggered into her bedroom. She allowed her eyes to browse the expanse of his chest, the chest hair spreading over firm pecs and tapering down to the six-pack of abs. And lower. To the impressive member of his anatomy hanging temptingly between two thick, muscular thighs. Raising her gaze to his face, she found his mouth hitched into a sideways smile, his hair mussed, and his stubble prominent.

She stared, smiling.

He just stood there and let her stare, smiling back.

"Did you want to—"

"I should get going," he said at the same time.

"Oh, of course." So he didn't want to stay. She tried not to be hurt by that, and really, she wasn't. She did feel exposed, however, and tugged the sheet higher, tucking it under her armpits.

"I, uh… Thanks." His smile was less easy, and his sentiment was…strange.

"You're welcome." Her sentiment, she found, was equally strange.

He gathered his clothes, pulling on his boxers and snapping the waistband against his flat stomach, pulling on his slacks, and buttoning up his shirt. By the time he ran his hands through his hair, she was full-on regretting that he was leaving so soon. She wanted to ask what he was doing this weekend, but bit back the urge.

"You gonna be okay here, recovering by yourself?" he asked, and it sounded like good-bye.

"Somehow I'll manage." Cupping a pillow, she curled into it and wished for a moment she had the courage to ask him to stay. Regardless of her fears, of what lingered between them, he'd feel better than this stupid pillow. And the pillow would not wake her and want morning sex.

Sigh.

He leaned over and pressed his lips to hers, squeezing one butt cheek as he did. "See you, McIntire."

Asking when would be needy so she didn't. Instead she said, "See you" and closed her eyes, refusing to watch him go. "Lock up before you go."

It was what he'd told her after their night together, and he didn't argue. Instead, he took the stairs, called out a low, rumbling "good night", and closed the door behind him.

Then the house was quiet.

And Lily was alone.

Chapter Sixteen

He'd wanted to stay Friday night. Wanted to tuck Lily beneath her blankets, pull her against his body, and fall asleep with her wrapped in his arms. Then he realized he needed to man the hell up before he sent her running for the hills. She was twitchy and this was new. As grateful as he was to have her in bed again, he didn't want to spook away the opportunity for it to happen again.

Never in his life had he been this careful. Then again, never before had he worried about spooking a woman. Before, if they got spooked, then hip-hip-hooray. After his failed relationship with Annie, girls could come, just so long as coming was followed by *going*. With Lily it was different. *He* was different. In a good way. Or at least, he thought it was a good way. Leaving her in bed alone Friday night made him feel nothing but shitty.

Reginald London was not wrong about Marcus being good at poker. He had a great poker face. Usually he smiled the entire time. Laughed his way through a bluff. Kind of like life. But where Lily was concerned, he was beginning to fear he'd shown too many of his cards way too soon.

She'd seen his hand all right. Actually, she'd seen every last inch of him, and he'd seen every last inch of her. It should have been enough, but it wasn't. She wasn't a conquest. This wasn't about getting laid, getting the girl temporarily.

He was beginning to worry this was about getting the girl *permanently*. After saying "never again," something in him was ready to try. After two years of crushing on Lily, dating other women, seeing Lily at the office the next day, and regretting the temporary fling, he knew what the end of the road looked like. And with any woman other than Lily in his arms, it looked a lot like misery.

From what he knew about her, the most important part of this was that Clive and Joanie never found out. That would be a challenge after what happened at their house during the London cocktail party, but Marcus was a convincing guy. He wasn't ready to cede yet. Even with Clive giving him the stink eye in the break room Monday afternoon.

"Seriously. We were arguing and didn't want to disturb the party," Marcus insisted, topping off his mug of coffee and mixing in a teaspoon of creamer. Eventually, if they kept seeing each other, they'd have to tell their friends, but for now, it wasn't any of their business. Clive was the hardest to convince, but if he had him, he had Joanie. Joanie, while incredibly intelligent, also had her mind on about nineteen different things at the same time. She was a lovable scatterbrain, and not always the most observant.

"Arguing." Clive leaned against the countertop, arms crossed, unimpressed.

"You know how we are." Marcus put the spoon in the sink and headed for the copy room. Clive followed. "Sorry if we ruined your party by running out, but it was for the best."

"What were you arguing about?" Clive asked.

Marcus turned and gave his buddy a planned eye roll. "Hawaii."

Clive nodded as if he wasn't surprised. "She doesn't want to go with you."

"Of course she doesn't." Actually, she hadn't really said one way or the other. When he told her the story he'd spun for Clive and Joanie last week, she'd sort of mumbled a response that may have been in the affirmative. He supposed he should see if she meant it or not, but now didn't feel like the right time.

Clive stopped short of following him into the copy room. Good thing, too. Marcus had nothing to copy. "Lunch today?"

"Uh, no thanks, I'm catching up on email."

"Suit yourself." He turned his head. "Lily, lunch?"

Marcus couldn't see her, but heard her approaching as she answered, "I have a lunch date."

"Oh. Okay then. Joanie!" Clive called across the hall. She answered with an "I know! I'm coming!"

"Enjoy your date, Lily," Clive told her, and Marcus came to the doorway in time to see the Camerons leave the building and Lily walking toward him, papers in hand.

"Hey, Marcus," she said brightly.

"Hi. I told Clive we were arguing at his house and that's why we left."

Her eyebrows crawled up her forehead. "And he believed you."

"Is it that hard to believe?"

She shrugged a shoulder and wouldn't look at him. He wanted to touch her, to pull her lips to his and say something teasing and sexy, then kiss her until she melted into him. Even with Joanie and Clive gone, and the temp off today, he was holding back until she explained her "lunch date."

"What are you working on today?" he asked instead.

"Oh, this and that. No big projects, just the little ones that require a lot of attention and a fast turnaround."

"Nice," he said, hating this how-is-the-weather conversation. It felt forced.

"Go back to the mansion yet?" she asked.

He shook his head. "Not yet. You?"

She shook her head. "I don't think I'll be going back."

"Not even if I dared you?"

She gave him a small smile as she fed her papers into the copier and pressed a button. "Especially not if you dared me."

"So." He put his coffee down on a table, watching the machine spit out copies. "You're...you have a lunch date."

"Mm-hmm," she said, far too casually for his liking. "Same guy that I'm going with to the RSD dinner." Her eyes trailed to the side. "Hope that won't be awkward."

"You *hope* that won't be awkward." Was he missing something major here? What had happened after he left her satisfied in her bed Friday? Did she get a call from an ex? Did she decide to end things with Marcus and not tell him?

"I mean...you don't mind, right?"

Jaw clenched, he leaned forward. "I mind, McIntire."

"Oh, bummer." Her blue eyes widened. "I was going to do that no-panty thing that you asked me to do."

His brow went down, his brain in Neanderthal mode. "What?"

"You, dummy. You're my lunch date. And my RSD dinner date."

Oh. Sweet.

"You'll pay for that."

"I hope so." She grinned.

He took the two steps separating them, lowered his face. Against her lips, he said, "Missed your mouth."

"It's only been two days."

Didn't he know it. "How did you sleep?"

"Fitfully." Her arms came up to drape around his neck, and he stepped in closer, palming her hips.

"Seriously? I would think you would've passed out, slept like the dead."

"What about you? How did you sleep?"

Not well. He'd wanted to be with her in her bed. He wanted her right now.

"When are we coming out of the closet?" he asked.

She chuckled. "You mean out of the pantry?"

"Yeah. When?" he pressed.

Her smile fell, and her arms tightened the slightest bit. She straightened, somehow managing to come away from him so that her shirt was no longer brushing his. "Don't you like no one knowing?"

"What about the RSD dinner this weekend? What is your plan there?"

"I told you, I'm not wearing panties."

"Which I appreciate, but what…we both show stag?"

"Worried about your reputation?" she teased.

"McIntire, quit jerking me around."

"Oh, but you like it." Her hand snaked between their bodies and cupped his crotch. His body bucked. His brain blanked. "Don't you?"

He ran his hands up her rib cage to just under her breasts. "You're distracting me on purpose."

She continued her erotic massage. "Yes, I am. What are you going to do about it?"

"Let you."

"I have unfinished business with you," she said, sliding his zipper down. "And I always finish what I start."

With the copier whirring away in the background, Lily sank to her knees and tore open his pants. He managed to back them out of sight from the front door, and hoped to God they'd hear if someone came into the building.

• • •

"You steal one more piece of my chicken, Black, and I am going to throttle you!" Lily raised her eyebrows and gave him the sternest expression she could manage. Part of that was for show. The other part was sincere. She would appreciate if he stopped eating her food.

He grinned, stuck his chopsticks into her paper container, and came out with another piece of chicken—which he then put in his mouth and chewed merrily while making moaning noises.

She turned to Joanie. "Are you seeing this?"

"Come on, guys. It's going on nine o'clock, and Joanie and I would like to go home and have crazy, hot, monkey sex on the sofa."

"Clive!" Joanie's face went pink.

"Okay, the kitchen counter," Clive corrected.

"I apologize for my husband." Joanie shook her head and dug into her noodles, and while she was a little red with embarrassment, she didn't look all that upset. Clive may be teasing about the *where*, but Lily had no doubts her best friends had an active love life. It was admirable really. They'd been married for seven years, and showed no signs they'd been together more than seven months.

"I suppose you're right, dear," Clive said. "It's rude to brag about my awesome sex life to two people who may or may not be getting any."

Worst timing ever. Lily had just taken a big bite. A big bite that also had a very big sliver of red pepper in it. Now she was coughing, and the pepper was burning her throat. Marcus stood from his chair to come to her aid. She waved him off frantically, able to catch her breath, as she reached for her Diet Coke and took a hearty sip.

"I'm fine," she croaked.

"I should get Clive home. If he continues to act like this toward our friends, the courteous thing to do is to remove him from your presence." Joanie stood from the conference table and began clearing the takeout containers. "Are you two going to keep working? If not, we can start again in the morning."

"You know me," Marcus said from beside Lily. He placed his palms on the table next to her, leaning over her and saturating the air with that delicious male scent of his. "I love to burn the midnight oil."

"Not me. I have to go home, pet my neighbor's cat, feed my goldfish, and heat a cup of soup for one." She gave Clive a sad smile. He gave her one back...but not like he was apologetic. No, he gave her a smile as if he knew more than he was letting on. He flicked a look to Marcus, and that smile broadened to a grin.

Interesting.

Her eyes went to her best friend, but she saw nothing on Joanie's face that said she had any clue what was happening. Then Lily snapped her attention to her immediate right, where Marcus stood over her, looking innocent, when clearly, he was not. He'd told her earlier that Clive had bought the "arguing" excuse, but to her, Clive looked unconvinced.

It wasn't easy, but Lily kept her comments to herself while her friends gathered their things and made their way out of the conference room. Marcus locked them out of the building while Lily cut through the hallway, building steam as she went. He swaggered his very fine ass in her direction, and she stepped out of her office, held up a finger, and poked him square in the chest.

"You said Clive bought it."

"He did." His thick eyebrows slammed down. "At least, I thought he did."

She put her hands on her hips. Marcus was an intimidating figure, and took up most of the narrow hallway. "Then why was he looking at me like he knew exactly what's been happening between us?"

"Between you and Clive?"

"Stop joking for a second." She put a palm on Marcus's chest and shoved. He didn't move. "You know I mean between you and me!"

"What *is* happening between you and me?" He stepped closer, leaning over her, looking far too serious. She wanted to eat her words and ask him to keep joking. Joking Marcus was easier than Intense Marcus. No less sexy, though.

"He—he just looks very in the know." She hedged, backing up another step but keeping her palm spread over his very solid pectorals.

"There's a reason for that. And it's your fault." Marcus advanced another step, looming over her now. She was trying her hardest to stay upset, but her resolve was crumbling like stale crackers. Her traitorous body responded, her nipples hardening and poking the thin material of her bra and silk shirt. She clenched her thighs as she studied his firm mouth, her knees wobbling as she attempted to stand her ground. "Clive is very observant," he continued. "He knows damn well what a satisfied woman looks like. And you"—he wrapped one broad hand around her hip and tugged her against his very solid thighs—"look like a satisfied woman."

She opened her mouth to argue, but produced no words at all. Usually this would be the point where he would kiss her. But he didn't. This near to him, her sexual frustration was reaching its peak.

"Not your fault." He twirled a piece of her hair around his finger and his expression softened. "You're killing me in this proper little suit," he said, skating a heated look over her shirt. "My place or yours?"

She swallowed thickly, the hand against his chest beginning to sweat. "I-I'm busy."

"You're gonna be," he said, smiling. "Need to know what bed you're gonna be in, though. Bringing my A game."

"Don't you think—?"

"About you underneath me? Only every other minute. Now answer me, or else I'll throw you on the nearest desk."

Heat burst onto her cheeks. He noticed.

"Oh, really?" He smiled down at her.

"No, that's not…um. The bed is fine." She shook her head, realizing the futility of arguing with him. It was like her vocal chords were in cahoots with her hormones. Not a single part of her body disagreed with his desk suggestion. She let out a blustery sigh.

"Resistance is futile."

"No shit," she grumbled.

"Come on, McIntire. Live a little."

"I did. In the copier room earlier."

"Live a little *more*." He was smiling and looking so damned gorgeous that she couldn't help smiling back. "My desk or yours?"

"My desk is—*eep!*"

He didn't let her finish, scooping her into his arms and carrying her into his office and kicking the door closed. Arms looped around his neck, her eyes went to his desk, covered with his computer, phone, and everything else.

"Other desk," he said, tipping his head at the six-foot table against the wall. The wide surface was clear of any papers, pencils, or clutter of any kind.

She locked eyes with Marcus and she realized why the smile slid across her face. Something about him made her… happy. Just plain happy. It was as simple and as complicated as that.

"Did you set the alarm?" she asked as he plopped her down onto the desk. She spread her hands over the surface. She didn't like to break rules…usually. She didn't get a weird rush at being deviant.

"Why, worried somebody might catch us?" His smile suggested he wouldn't.

"If Clive or Joanie forget something and try to come back…"

When she didn't finish her sentence, he said, "Yes?"

"You really don't care if they know, do you?"

"I care about one thing." He fell silent, and she braced for him to say something tender and warm. Something that would make her feel a little too much in the general area of her heart. But she lucked out, because a second later his smirk clicked into place and he said, "Making you come."

Chapter Seventeen

That was not what he cared about. Okay, it *was* what he cared about. He cared about making her come a lot. But he also cared about something else.

Her.

He cared about her enough that he was going to continue this insane idea to keep things quiet even though he didn't like lying to his friends. But not for long. And he needed to let her know that. She sat, legs kicking over the edge of the desk, hair rolling over her shoulders, white shirt doing nothing to hide her peaked nipples...

He'd let her know later. After desk sex.

"Don't rip my buttons this time. I still have to drive home."

Why, *why* did rod-up-her-ass, Lily McIntire do it for him whenever she was being rigid? Probably because he knew she really wasn't. As a matter of fact, under his hands and his mouth, she was downright pliant. Like melted peanut butter.

Mmm, too bad he didn't have that in his food cabinet at work.

"Okay, you take it off." He smoothed his palm over her bare calf down to one rather demure heeled shoe, which he removed and tossed over his shoulder. It thudded to the floor behind him.

"Do you have any idea how much those cost?" Her brow furrowed, fingers hovering over the top button of her blouse.

"Nope." He moved to the other leg, slid that shoe off, and tossed it into the metal trash can next to his desk. It hit the side with a *clang*. "Now ask me if I care."

She gave him a scolding look, but since she was undoing her shirt buttons – and not slowly – he didn't mind. Not that he'd mind anyway. Lily's scolding looks were kind of cute.

"Did you get the salon plans approved?" She continued working her buttons, her attention on her shirt. By the time she was pulling it off her shoulders, he was thoroughly perplexed by this turn of conversation. "I was thinking about it today and wondering if it wouldn't be nice to have a drink station where customers could help themselves. Coffee, tea, maybe a few nice wine selections…"

He held up a hand to stop her. "Are you under the assumption that talking about salon floor plans turns me on? Because it does not."

"No, I'm not assuming anything. I'm just making conversation."

His eyes went to a decidedly plain white bra that somehow still looked sexy on her. "Why?"

"Because you said you wanted to work tonight."

"On getting you naked," he said. "But I couldn't exactly blurt that out in the meeting, now could I?"

Before she could argue, which she was poised to do, he stopped the words in her throat by reaching behind her back, flicking the clasp on her bra, and sliding the straps halfway down her arms. "I love that they're peach."

"What?" She blinked down at her bare breasts.

"Your nipples." He ran his thumb over one, watching it harden further under his touch. "They're perfect."

"If you're trying to prove you're good at seduction, there's really no need."

He moved her slim-fitting skirt high on her thighs. High enough to spread her legs and insert himself in between. "Careful, McIntire, that was almost a compliment."

He lowered his head and took a perfect peach nipple into his mouth. Her hand went to his hair, spearing through the strands as her back arched and she pressed her breasts against his face.

This was better. Better than her being combative, better than trying to figure out what came next. Just better. Anything in life was better with his mouth on Lily.

He tongued her breasts while slipping his fingers into her cotton panties, and turning her inside out with precisely placed strokes. Then he dragged them from her legs, leaving them dangling from one of her ankles.

Lily was *exquisite*, with her skirt hiked to her waist, her head thrown back, strawberry waves spilling over the edge of the desk. She canted her hips and he took advantage of her throes, leaving her for mere seconds to roll on a condom. Then he returned, sliding into her deep, and loving the pleased sound that escaped her mouth.

She was every fantasy come true. From the skirt, to the panties, to her breasts bouncing with his each forward thrust. She'd rested one foot on his shoulder, giving him a hell of a view between her legs. Her other leg was wrapped securely around his waist, pulling him in because she wanted him closer.

Closer.

Desk sex was fantastic, but there was one problem. He couldn't reach her mouth. And he needed her mouth. Unable to keep his distance any longer, he palmed her back, lifting her. Her lust-filled eyes were hooded, her pupils wide, her breath fanning out and blowing the fine strands of her hair.

His heart constricted, feeling so much for her in this moment, he wasn't one hundred percent sure she couldn't read it on his face.

"Dammit, McIntire," he growled. She looped her arms around his neck and gave him a pleased smile. "Kiss me."

• • •

She was unraveling. Marcus had started at her nipples, moved to sliding his fingers between her thighs, and now he was kissing her within an inch of her life.

Desk sex was *good.*

With Marcus, her mind filled in.

Dangerous thought, that. She swore after her last office relationship, she'd never have another. Granted, she hadn't had the office relationship literally *in an office.* Marcus scooted her to the edge of the desk.

His arms wrapped around her, her body molded against his, and his eyes unerringly focused on hers. He took up every ounce of space in her immediate space, filled her vision, filled her body. That's the way it had been with him. And she couldn't find it within herself to complain.

The next pull and push of his hips caused pressure to build deep in her core. "Marcus," she moaned into his mouth. Her thighs clamped.

"That's it, Lil." He pounded into her again, knowing just what she needed. "Come, baby. I've got you."

He did have her. He had her cradled in those big arms. But then, she was cradling him between her legs, too. They were holding onto each other.

"I've got you," he repeated.

At his next thrust, she let go—let go while she held onto him, her pulse skyrocketing, her breath shallow, her mind a complete and utter haze.

His release was on the heels of hers, and she enjoyed his orgasm almost as much as she enjoyed her own—the low sounds he made, his masculine scent curling in her nostrils, the way he felt inside her when he let himself go.

Incredible.

He held her to him while his breaths slowed, then he released her, laying her on the table. He kissed her chest, her collarbone, the side of her neck, then placed a soft kiss on the center of her mouth. She fingered his short hair, pushing it away from his forehead, and gave him a thoroughly satisfied smile.

His smile matched hers, lips parting over straight, white teeth, that dimple buried under a few days' worth of growth. She raked her fingers through his stubble, loving the feel of it now that it was slightly soft.

"Growing a beard?" she asked.

"Want me to?"

She raised a brow. "Would you if I asked?"

He didn't hesitate. "Yeah."

Then he kissed her, and the silly romantic inside her wondered what else he'd do if she asked.

It was a tantalizing thought.

• • •

Cold chicken tasted better when Lily fed it to him.

He opened his mouth and she threw in a piece. She fished out another piece from the container and he opened his mouth, but she kept that bite for herself. He snatched her wrist and pulled her fingertips into his mouth, sucking the sauce off each one.

"Mm. We should eat every meal like this," she said.

They were perched on the desk they'd made love on—er, *banged* on, he reminded himself tersely. Thanks to the solid craftsmanship of the Amish, it'd held them both, not wobbling in the least. He'd known it was a good purchase.

Lily redressed but he didn't have the heart to tell her she'd buttoned her blouse crooked. Her hair was a frizzy tornado, her bare feet were folded under her, and her panties were in his pocket. She'd tried to wrestle them from his grip earlier and failed.

He hadn't let her have them back, insisting this would be good practice for the RSD dinner. Now that he had the prize in his pocket, he was considering slipping them to her under the table during tomorrow's meeting. That'd be fun.

"What are you smiling about?" she asked.

"Come home with me."

Shit. So much for manning up.

She shoveled a bite of food into her mouth with the chopsticks. Gesturing to her chewing mouth, she shrugged like she couldn't answer.

"You're doing that on purpose," he pointed out.

She spent a few more seconds chewing, swallowing, and running her tongue over her teeth.

"Seriously?"

She licked her lips, wiped her fingers along the corners of her mouth, and then said, "Okay."

"Okay?" He was so shocked by a positive response, he nearly toppled off the desk.

She nodded.

"Okay." He grabbed his keys from his desk. "Grab your stuff. Let's go."

He waited while she retrieved her purse and they left together, Marcus setting the alarm and locking up behind him.

"I'm driving," he said.

"I can't leave my car here." She was halfway to her cherry-red compact already. "Joanie and Clive will wonder what happened."

"And?"

"And...they will think you gave me a ride home."

"Then they'll be right. I'm giving you a ride to my home."

He saw the worry on her face and paced over to where she stood. "Lil, what are you scared of?"

"I...I've done this before. Had a relationship with a guy I worked with."

He frowned.

"A long time ago," she added. "When I worked at Lawson and Becker. It didn't end well."

"Okay." News to him. He knew she'd come from L&B before she worked here, but he didn't know she'd left because of a guy.

"So, you know." She averted her gaze. "I just don't want things to end badly between us. For either of us."

He nodded. Understandable.

He pocketed his keys and palmed her neck, moving her hair over her shoulder. When he pulled her close, she wrapped her arms around his waist. He liked her holding on to him and wished she'd do it a little more. "You can trust me."

"It's not that I don't," she murmured, resting her cheek against his chest.

He kissed the top of her head.

"I just... I don't want to try and explain. This is ours. Like the mansion. That's ours, too. No one would believe what we experienced there. And I don't want to explain it." She pulled away from him to look up.

Damn. He got that. Here he'd thought she was ashamed of him. Still... "Fine. But this is a short-term plan. I'll give you until this weekend, and then you're going to show up at the RSD dinner, proudly cling to me like...well, like you're clinging to me now."

"Marcus."

"I'm not going to put on a show for the dinner. Make up reasons why I don't have a date instead of telling everyone the truth—that you're on my arm. You're with me."

She let go of him. "That makes me so nervous."

"Why?"

She hoisted an eyebrow. "Almost as nervous as you giving a thank-you speech to over three hundred members of the—"

He pressed his fingertips over her mouth, and then re-placed them with his lips. She'd successfully changed the subject. Part of the reason his heart rate had escalated was due to imagining three hundred pairs of eyes on him while he bumbled his way through a speech that was supposed to fill fifteen minutes.

Fifteen minutes.

That was how much time he'd approximated he'd spent with his head between Lily's thighs the other night, which proved that time was well and truly relative. It'd flown then, with her sounds of pleasure swirling the air. But this morning when he'd practiced his speech in the mirror—yeah, not so much. His throat had closed off at six minutes, and he'd been sweating and shaky.

Not cool.

And definitely not attractive.

If he wanted to show up at the dinner and claim this amazing woman as his own, he'd better make sure he wasn't a pansy at the podium.

"We can practice," she said. "Tonight."

Sweat beaded on his brow. "I have other plans for tonight."

"Then we'll practice after we um…" She seemed to choose the words carefully. "Work out."

"Work out?"

"Yep." She unlocked her car and lifted the handle. "I'm counting this as exercise."

He let her have that…and the fact that she was driving herself. "My place, McIntire."

"See you there, Black."

• • •

He swiped his forehead with his hand, swallowing thickly and feeling like his airway was partially closed. "It's hot in here."

"It's not hot. You're hot, though." Lily leaned on a pile of pillows on his slate gray sheets, her naked body covered with a sheet, looking sated and relaxed, her hair a bigger mess than earlier.

He felt like he'd worked out—run a marathon, actually. His muscles were loose and spent, his mind was clear. She was going to regret making this bet.

He stood at the end of the bed and lifted his notecards. "You're sure you're ready to lose?"

"I'm not going to lose. You're going to choke."

He narrowed his eyes. Competing with Lily at work had always been fun. Competing with her in the bedroom was even more fun. After he'd pulled out of her body, while they lay next to each other on the bed, she had turned that competitive spirit on him. "I'll bet you can't get through your speech right now." Which of course, he'd contested. She didn't know him. Sex cleared his mind of cobwebs and fuzz.

"I'm not going to choke," he told her now. "You'd better get your dancing shoes on."

Because the other side of that bet was that when he won, she'd have to do a little dance to a song of his choosing. Without any clothes on.

"I think you'll be crawling back in here with your tail between your legs. Clock's ticking, Black." She crossed her arms over her chest. "Just remember, fifteen minutes is a quarter of an hour."

And now she was psyching him out. "Playing dirty."

"I learned from the best."

That was fair. He tossed his notecards on his dresser and tugged the waistband of his jeans. Yeah, he'd pulled on his jeans. He couldn't give a speech in the nude, even in the privacy of his bedroom. It was too much like the nightmare he had of showing up naked at the dinner.

"I'm timing you." She adjusted his nightstand clock so she could see it and he felt his stomach toss.

Closing his eyes, he took a deep, deep breath. *Think what you'll get when you win. Lily dancing naked.* As motivations went, having Lily naked was a good one. He opened his eyes and rolled his shoulders. Turned his head to both sides and cracked his neck.

"So, Donald Duck walks into a pants store." He cleared his throat, waited for the laugh.

Lily pursed her lips. "Was that...was that supposed to be funny?"

"You're supposed to start with a joke." He grimaced at her.

She grimaced back. "Don't start with that joke. Start with something simple."

Sucking in a breath, he was careful to keep from frowning, like she'd advised him the night he'd practiced at the mansion. He pulled his shoulders back and said evenly, "Ladies and gentlemen..."

• • •

Crap. She was *so* going to lose.

She tore her eyes off shirtless, sexy Marcus to eye the clock. He continued his speech with fervor and with his usual cocky air of confidence. If he hadn't admitted he was nervous, she never could have been able to tell.

"Furthermore…" He held up a finger and smiled. "I'd like to thank Lily McIntire, who will now be forced to shimmy her sweet ass out of my bed and shake her groove thing to the soothing sounds of AC/DC's 'Shook Me All Night Long.'"

She reached behind her head and threw a pillow. He caught it.

"Don't be a sore loser."

She folded her arms over her chest and pouted. Why had she promised a nude private dance?

"I'm kidding." Marcus climbed onto the bed and leaned on his fists. Relief relaxed her shoulders until he added, "I won't make you dance to AC/DC."

He tore back the sheets and flipped to his back, jostling the bed. "Let's see your moves, McIntire."

"Rain check?" she tried.

"Not on your life."

"What if…what if we do something else instead?" She palmed his crotch and his hips rose to meet her hand. But he still did not break.

"If you'd like to make that your finishing number," he said with a grin, "fine by me."

. . .

Lily slipped out of bed and gave him the stink eye as she crossed the room. Her body was a beautiful sight in the low lamplight. He enjoyed watching her fleshy bottom move across the room, and the way her nipples peaked in the cooler air of his bedroom.

He reached for his iPhone and chose an acoustic song, not overly romantic and cheesy, just something to give her a beat to sway to. And to his surprise and pleasure, she swayed. She rocked her hips, closed her eyes, and rolled those delicate shoulders. By the time she scooped her hair off her neck and piled it behind her head, he was physically unable to lie there and not touch her for another second.

He pushed off the bed, still wearing his jeans and hard as the night was long, and her eyes flew open. Hands on her hips, he pulled her close, pressing the soft globes of her breasts to his bare chest. Her slim fingers swept along his ribs and they danced like that for a few seconds before he took her hand in his and placed the other on his shoulder.

She laughed. "We look ridiculous."

"Huh-uh." He turned so she could see them in the mirrored closet doors. "Amazing." His hand palmed her butt and he watched her eyes follow the movement in their reflection. "Tell me, Ms. McIntire."

"Ohh, formal," she said, tilting her chin up at him.

He took advantage of her nearness and kissed her lips, moving his hips with hers to the steady beat of the song. "Would you let me pick you up for the RSD dinner? I was thinking of renting a limo."

That laugh again. It'd be the death of him. He'd thought arguing with Lily was fun, but tickling her funny bone? Infinitely *more* fun.

"How very low key of you," she said.

"Well, we're coming out. May as well do it in style."

Her hand slipped from his shoulder to his chest. She stopped dancing. "What will everyone think?"

"Who cares?" he said. And really, who *did* care? "I'm a kickass designer. So are you. People hire us to design, not because we do or do not sleep together."

She was quiet for a beat, then said, "I guess you're right."

"So?"

"Okay." Her smile wasn't full force, but he'd take it. "You can pick me up. But not"—she poked him in the stomach—"in a limo."

He bent and scooped her up, that incredible butt resting in both his palms, and dropped her onto his bed. He undid his button fly jeans, tossed them aside, and then joined her.

They made love again and this time she was on top, her breasts swaying in front of his face, her hair cascading down her back. Afterward, she collapsed next to him, rolled over, and pressed that sweet backside against his front.

He held her tightly, one arm around her, and listened to her breathing even out. The soft scent of her hair invaded his senses as he tried to remember if he'd ever made a better decision than seducing Lily at Willow Mansion.

He couldn't think of one.

Chapter Eighteen

Lily stared out the passenger side window, chewing on her bottom lip. Marcus could see she was nervous—if not by the lip-chewing thing, then in the stiffness of her posture. And he could feel it to, in the clamminess dampening their linked hands.

He pulled his sports car into a parking space outside the convention center, killed the engine, and turned his head. "I'm the one who's supposed to be nervous."

She jumped slightly, like he'd startled her, her delicate throat moving as she swallowed. Other than her apparent nerves, she looked drop-dead gorgeous in a clingy emerald green dress (short, as per his request) and high, high shoes. When she'd opened her front door, he'd forgotten how to speak for a moment. His eyes had coasted along her beautiful, pale breasts, bursting out of the deep *V* formed by the wraparound dress. Truth told, those breasts were still distracting him, and if that wasn't enough, he had the no-panty thing to contend with.

"What are you wearing under that dress?"

"Nothing but a new bikini wax," she purred.

God help him.

But their playful banter had died halfway to the conference center, and she'd fallen silent for the remainder of the drive.

"You okay?" Out of habit, his eyes dipped down to her cleavage before meeting her gaze.

"Sure. Of course." A nod of her head, then, "Are you?" She let go of his hand to straighten his bow tie.

The annual dinner was formal, and no joke. Industry brass would be there—people from big name firms, other designers, owners, and high-paying customers. Hell, Reginald London's firm was presenting Marcus with his award tonight.

"I'll be better once I'm off that stage," he told her, meaning it. He may have pulled a win out of his back pocket when he'd practiced with her in his bedroom, but his mind had been firmly on winning her nude dancing.

"You'll be great." Her smile was not genuine, and he didn't like when she wasn't blunt with him.

"Dammit, Lily." He unbuckled and got of the car, walking around to her side. By the time he reached her door, she was climbing out. "What's the problem?"

"Excuse me." She sent a furtive look to the left then to the right.

"Who the hell are you looking for?" he asked, raising his arms in exasperation.

"No one. I just... Now that we're here, I think tonight is the wrong time to go public."

"Why?" He was done letting her off the hook.

"Because you have to concentrate on your speech."

"Lame."

"And I'd like the attention to be on you, not on us as a couple."

"Lily." He stepped close to her and she backed away, leaning against his freshly washed car. "We're not celebrities. I doubt anyone will notice beyond our circle of friends. I'm not planning on some massive PDA, I just don't want to have to think about holding your hand or not holding your hand, or eating off your plate if I want a bite of your dinner."

"I'm not sharing my dinner."

He ignored her attempt to distract him. "I mean it. I'm not going in there and putting on a show. We go in, arm in arm, and to hell with anyone who might have a problem with it." He palmed her jaw and leaned in.

She turned her head.

He dropped his arm and straightened. "Are you kidding me?"

"You bring a different girl here every year." Now she was angry, her eyebrows down, her voice raised slightly.

"Who cares? I'm here with you this year, McIntire."

A car pulled into the lot, its headlights cutting across the darkness, and her next words were quiet. "I care, Marcus. People talk. And the last thing I need are rumors bouncing around that I'm sleeping with the designer of the year to further my career."

"That's stupid." Who would give a shit if they were sleeping together? He was missing something. Some big piece of the puzzle wasn't sliding into place.

"Not my rules," she said.

"So, what? You want to go in separate? Leave separate?

Care to synchronize our watches or have a signal? I can pick you up a block away if you like."

"Thanks for taking me seriously."

He took a deep breath, pulling in a lot of patience and little oxygen, and then blew out a gusty sigh. They weren't going to resolve this in the few minutes before they walked in, clearly. And he didn't need the stress of Lily pissed at him when he had to remember not to faint on stage.

"Fine," he said, leaning against the car next to her, arms folded. "You first. I'll give you a few minutes."

"Thank you." To his complete dissatisfaction, she held her head high as she clipped inside and didn't spare him a single glance.

There was more going on here than she was saying. She wasn't confiding in him, and that pissed him off as much as it concerned him.

. . .

"There you are!" Joanie. Smiling, happy, lovely Joanie. Lily's best friend swished over to her. She was draped in a stunning blue, floor-length gown. Clive, looking dapper in a black tuxedo, followed behind his wife, two glasses of champagne in his hands. Joanie hugged Lily briefly, then peered over her shoulder as she pulled away. "Where's Marcus?"

"Marcus?"

"Yeah, guy you work with," Clive said blandly. "My best friend." He handed over a flute to Joanie and offered Lily the other.

She accepted, and filled the awkward space between the question and her lame answer by taking a sip. "Not my turn to watch him, ha-ha."

Her eyes swept the room in search of Emmett. Before, when she'd agreed to let Marcus drive her to the dinner, she'd been able to brush off the fact that Emmett would be here, and that he'd see her on Marcus's arm. She'd liked the idea of it, actually. Then, tonight, as she pinned her hair up and spritzed perfume over her classy but revealing cocktail dress, she played another possible scenario in her head. Emmett seeing her with Marcus and telling Reginald London that Cameron Designs as a firm was wholly unsuited for the task of designing their superstore. And after Reginald had witnessed Marcus and Lily leaving the Camerons' house together…what would he think? Of course, while she was having her little panic attack, she also considered the possibility that Reginald wouldn't care at all. Joanie and Clive were married, and obviously sleeping together.

But the past still stung her like angry wasps—the memory of Emmett betraying her, the way his claim that she'd been dishonest had completely tanked her career. In that moment, in L&B's office with Ira Becker, she'd been made to feel like a cheap hanger-on rather than the brilliant designer behind the work that had landed them a huge account.

And it was that memory, and Emmett's dig of "more boobs than brains," that made her chicken out.

"Miss? Your coat?" A man in a smart black suit held out his hands and Lily peeled her coat away, feeling exposed now that she was here. In reality, she was showing no more skin than anyone else, but the airy reminder of her lack of undergarments made her feel like she had a sign announcing that she wasn't wearing anything under her dress.

"Oh, that dress!" Joanie exclaimed as the man took her

coat. "You look absolutely gorgeous. Marcus will die."

Lily blinked at her friend, stunned.

"Come on, Lil," Clive said, plunging his hands into his pockets. "How much longer are you two gonna pretend not to be dating?"

"We know, sweetie," Joanie said, when Lily didn't respond. "Ever since the mansion you two have been behaving like horny teenagers."

"Arguably," Lily mumbled after swallowing another drink, "we've always behaved like teenagers with each other."

"True."

"So, it's official, you and Marcus are doing it like rabbits," Clive blurted.

"Crass!" Joanie slapped her husband in the arm. Then she wrapped that hand around his elbow and stood close to him. "How could you not tell us, though?" she asked Lily. "We're your best friends."

There was no way she could hide this for much longer anyway. "Emmett."

Understanding dawned in Joanie's eyes. "Oh. I forgot about him."

If only Lily could do the same.

"Emmett Webster?" Clive asked, his brow dented. "I just met him. One of London's guys. I think he's the head of marketing or something."

"Or something," Lily muttered guiltily. "He's the reason I left L&B."

"Shit." Clive's jaw tightened. "He's the asshole who—"

"Honey." Joanie ran a soothing hand over Clive's tuxedo sleeve. "Not the time. Or the place."

"You don't want Marcus to know," Clive said, still

looking unhappy.

"His speech," Lily said. "He's ready. He's good. But I'm worried if he found out, he'd be murderous and then who knows…"

Clive gave her a slow nod. "Since I feel murderous, I think you may be right."

"So, we'll keep it to ourselves tonight. No biggie," Joanie said.

"Don't worry, Lil," Clive said. "We won't let that asshole rile you."

His eyes went past Lily's shoulder and she turned to see Marcus striding through the front doors. He looked so good tonight. So, *so* good. He wore a tux better than any man in the room. With those broad shoulders filling his jacket and his almost-black hair styled, his former stubble more a neatly trimmed beard… He'd grown it because she'd asked him to. Again, she wondered if he'd do just about anything for her.

Like come in here and pretend they weren't dating.

"There you guys are," Marcus said. His eyes briefly scanned down her dress and up again. "You scrub up nicely, McIntire." It was almost the complete opposite of what he'd said in her doorway. When she'd opened her front door to find him standing on her step with a bouquet of roses, he'd given her a reverent sweep of his eyes, followed by, *"Lily, my God. You're a vision."* Followed by the quip about her undergarments. To which she played into his talented hands perfectly. She missed that joking, sharp version of them. This version felt dull and sterile by comparison.

"Thanks," she said. "You look nice."

His lips pressed together, clearly displeased to carry on like this.

Then the shithead hit the fan.

Emmett Webster approached from across the room. He wore an off-the-rack suit on his medium frame, and a salesman's smile on his peach-fuzz face. She used to find him attractive. She still would, she supposed, if she hadn't known about the lying, forked tongue hiding behind his pearly teeth. His sharp, dark-blue eyes sliced down her body and up again and she tried not to feel self-conscious.

"As I live and breathe," he said.

She was aware of Marcus taking a step closer to her. She didn't think he knew who Emmett was, but she could be wrong. Suddenly, she wished she hadn't insisted on this charade. If Marcus knew Joanie and Clive knew about them, he'd have slipped an arm around Lily and she could have leaned into his strength… Then again, Emmett would probably have said something then there'd be a brawl in the center of the dinner.

She pictured Marcus punching Emmett out. It was not a bad picture. But definitely a bad idea. Marcus deserved the spotlight for his accomplishments.

"Reginald pointed you out." Emmett smiled at Marcus, ignoring her now. He held out a hand and introduced himself. "Emmett Webster. I'll be handing out your award tonight on behalf of Mr. London. I wanted to extend personal congratulations. As a former designer, I appreciate your work. It'll be an honor, my friend."

Marcus's eyes were narrowed as he pumped the other man's hand twice. He didn't look as if he knew who Emmett was to Lily, or who he was at all, but she could tell by the bend of his eyebrows, Marcus didn't buy her smarmy ex's faux sentiments.

"Thanks," Marcus said. His hand found her lower back and she stood straighter. "My coworker, Lily McIntire, and the owners of Cameron Designs, Clive and Joanie Cameron."

"We've met," Emmett said to Clive. "Joanie, is it?" He shook her hand next and Joanie speared him with a look of contempt. He held a hand out to Lily. "Lily of the Valley. We've met before, too."

He would do that, wouldn't he? Blurt out that stupid nickname in front of everyone.

One of Marcus's eyebrows jumped, but other than that, he remained silent.

Their little reunion was interrupted by a voice crackling over the loudspeaker, asking everyone to take their seats.

"I'll see you up there," Emmett said to Marcus, and then he winked at Lily. "See you around."

Once he'd gone, she felt Marcus's dark gaze on her. "Lily of the Valley?"

"Um…inside joke. It's stupid." She clutched her champagne glass, watching Emmett go and wanting to tell Marcus everything. But now was not the time. "Tell you later."

Marcus fell into step next to her as they made their way across the room to their assigned table. White tablecloths with turquoise linen napkins and black confetti decorated the table.

Cameron Designs was seated with another small firm at a table close to the stage, no doubt because Marcus needed to be near by when he stepped up there. At least London and Emmett weren't seated at their table. She didn't know if she could politely endure her ex for more than a few minutes.

Just a few hours and then she'd tell Marcus the truth. After the dinner, after his speech, preferably after they'd stripped each other out of their fancy clothes.

Once she was naked against him, she'd tell him every-thing. And he'd understand. She knew he would.

• • •

The roast chicken was bland and the green beans under-cooked, but that wasn't why Marcus didn't eat much. Various members of the guild stepped up to the mic to speak, and he found himself imagining his turn. Imagining the hundreds of gazes locked on him... His stomach tossed like a rogue wave.

Clive and Joanie paid attention to the stage, and not to him and Lily. She sat to Marcus's left, Joanie on her left, Clive on Joanie's left. An older guy with a big gut and head full of graying hair sat to Marcus's right. He was cheery enough, but every breath he took sounded like a wheeze. And he was sweating profusely. Their table was up front, but they were out of range of the hot lights overhead. Marcus sent him a strained smile and prayed the guy wasn't about to have a heart attack.

After dinner and dessert, that was his cue. The intro-duction and presentation for designer of the year was next. Clearing his throat, he swept his napkin off his lap and dropped it next to the remainder of his cake.

Before he stood, Lily grasped his hand under the tablecloth. He stole a glance at Clive, who lifted an eyebrow before turning back to his cake. Joanie pecked something into her phone, paying them no mind.

"You've got this," Lily whispered, squeezing his hand. Then she leaned close, her warm breath tickling his ear, and whispered, "If you get nervous, just hang onto these." Then she turned her hand over in his and slipped something tiny and silky into his palm.

She pulled her hand away and picked up her fork, taking a bite of her chocolate cake while he tried to remember his speech...or his name. Everything blanked as he stuffed what he knew were Lily's missing panties into his pants pocket.

"You'll pay for that," he said under his breath, as he stood.

"Counting on it." She beamed up at him, and he could have kissed her. Would have, dammit, if not for them pretending they weren't together. He guessed the panties would have to do. "Good luck," she said brightly.

"Thanks, McIntire," he said, standing and pushing his chair in. "Not sure if that's helpful or not." Clive and Joanie echoed her sentiment of "good luck" and he thanked them, too, and then strode up the stairs behind the stage.

He held his shoulders back, feeling a lot like he did when he was in Little League—up to bat and sicker than a dog at the possibility of striking out.

But tonight, he wouldn't strike out. Hand in his pocket, he fingered the silky gift and eyed Lily, who was leaning over and saying something to Joanie.

He had this. He fucking *had it.*

His smile faded when he met Emmett Webster waiting in the wings. The guy just rubbed Marcus the wrong way. There was something untrustworthy about him. And he didn't like how he'd addressed Lily. The nickname seemed less an inside joke and more an insult.

"Ten minutes, they tell me," Emmett said, when Marcus made it over to where he was standing. "I'm going to say a few words about Reginald London Superstores, mention very briefly the grand opening date of the new store, then I'll introduce you as the man in charge who single-handedly got the win."

Emmett slapped Marcus's arm in what he guessed was supposed to be camaraderie.

"Cameron Designs as a team designed London's superstore," Marcus corrected. "Might want to downplay the single-handedly part."

"Yeah," Emmett agreed, but didn't sound agreeable, "but both you and I know the battle is won by the leader. And you are clearly the leader between you and Lily of the Valley."

Marcus's eyes narrowed. "Where did you two meet, again?"

"Oh, I used to be the lead designer at Lawson and Becker."

Marcus's blood pressure skyrocketed. Seriously, he could feel his blood boiling.

"Then you know how talented Lily is," Marcus said. "How well she can handle a presentation. She landed that account in the boardroom. The drawings were secondary."

"Oh, I know how well the woman can use her mouth, if you—" Emmett's words cut off with a choking sound—it was hard to speak with Marcus's hand wrapped around his throat.

Emmett's hands flew up and Marcus eased his grip, lowering his face and delivering a very clear threat. "How many of those teeth do you want to keep?"

The music started, Emmett's cue. *Fuck*. The timing was terrible. Half of him wanted to knock Emmett out and glide onto stage and introduce himself. Sending a bloody-nosed Emmett rolling down the back staircase would make Marcus feel a hell of a lot better…but he had more than himself to think about. Lily. Joanie and Clive.

He let go. Emmett began straightening his tie. "I'm guessing you two have a thing."

"None of your business what we have."

"Just a warning, man to man…"

Marcus loomed over him and Emmett backed into the curtain, ruffling it. The music swelled. "Get out there. Before I change my mind and hit you anyway."

Emmett straightened his jacket and nodded.

And Marcus closed his eyes and tried to reclaim his cool, and remember the words from his speech.

Chapter Nineteen

"When are you telling him?" Joanie asked after Marcus disappeared behind the stage.

"After." Lily smiled over at her friend. "I just wanted to send him up on that stage with nothing on his mind except for his speech." And the fact that he had her panties in his pocket. The other night when he practiced in front of her, he'd been confident and sure of himself. She wanted to give him a physical reminder that after his speech, she'd be naked and waiting for him. It helped, she guessed, since he'd walked behind the stage at a full strut.

The music continued for a few measured beats too long, and Lily began to worry...until Emmett stepped onto stage, lifting a hand to wave at the crowd. The jerk.

His introduction was brief, and sounded sincere enough. He held out an arm to introduce Marcus and Lily had to swipe her palms on her napkin when Marcus appeared, looking handsome and sexy, and just a smidge nervous.

"Come on, Black," she said to herself. *He's got this. He's totally got this.*

Marcus stepped on stage, confidence in his dark eyes, and waved one masculine hand at the audience. As he did, she took a look around the room to see the admiring smiles of his peers.

"I was going to start my speech with a Donald Duck joke, but my esteemed colleague, and partner at Cameron Design, Ms. Lily McIntire, suggested I don't lose the confidence of my audience right off the bat."

Everyone laughed. Right on point. He winked at her and continued smoothly. Damn. He did have this. He flowed from sentence to sentence with barely a pause, speaking clearly, making eye contact every so often. The slight waver in his voice at the start of the speech was gone after the audience laughed at his opening line. He was charming, grateful, and had definitely earned his place in the spotlight.

And in her heart, she realized in a flash.

Something about watching him from afar made her see him clearly. Made her not want to keep him far, or keep them a secret any longer. Made her want him on a permanent basis. Made her realize that while Emmett was her past… Marcus was her future. She loved everything about him.

He wrapped up his speech, earning a standing ovation to which Clive added a series of loud whistles. Marcus cradled the coveted crystal award in both hands, and Lily couldn't feel anything but pride that he'd been honored tonight.

"I'm gonna run to the ladies' room," Lily told Joanie, feeling overcome with emotion. She made it into the ladies' room and out before there was much of a line, then instead of going back to the table right away, walked across the room to the balcony overlooking the lawn.

The warm air of the conference room fell off her as the crisp autumn air abraded her skin and made goose bumps stand out on her arms. She took in the stars twinkling in the dark sky, welcoming the chill. The moon was full, lighting the grounds and making the stars seem pale by comparison.

From the balcony, she could see down the hill to the rest of Fantom, streetlights and headlights as cars crisscrossed the intersecting roads. She couldn't see Willow Mansion from here, but imagined she could. It was there, somewhere beyond the highway, and inside she pictured her discarded air mattress, Coleman lantern, and the heater, all sitting in the living room with who- or whatever had frightened her and Marcus out of the house.

Marcus, who'd rigged a speaker with a voice, she thought, shaking her head. The cheater. But still there was plenty they couldn't explain—them tumbling into bed together at the top of the list. She never would have slept with him otherwise, so in a way, she had Willow Mansion and that crazy dare to thank for finding the man who made her start thinking of her future again instead of flailing in the present.

Tonight, she'd tell him that. Tell him about Emmett. And then they could celebrate. With champagne and sex and plans for Hawaii. She turned on her heel to go back inside, a smile on her face and Marcus in her heart.

· · ·

Marcus stood and talked business with Reginald for a few minutes after his speech. As fun as it would have been to introduce Emmett Webster to his fist, Marcus grudgingly admitted to himself that he'd made the right decision. Reginald had turned his attention elsewhere, so Marcus headed for the bar. He needed a drink like his next breath.

During his chat with London, Marcus had put in a suggestion that Cameron Designs draw up a layout for the other superstore to open next fall. He knew the building London was refurbishing in Cincinnati. Marcus let Reginald know that he and Lily would personally head up the project to ensure it matched the current design of his first Ohio store. London was impressed, and with that groundwork laid, Marcus's gut told him Cameron Designs would be doing more for London in the future.

"Hey! There's our guy!" Joanie exclaimed, turning from the bar, wine in hand. Clive was there, too, with a glass of his own. She leaned in and said not that quietly, "We know about you and Lily. And we approve." Then she put a hand to her chest and blew out a breath. "God. That secret was killing me."

Marcus frowned. "You know?"

"We know," Clive said. "Now go find her so she can tell you. She didn't want to blow your big speech. Nice work, by the way."

"Thanks." But Marcus's mind was hooked on the fact that Lily was concerned about getting him through the speech. But her nerves over his speech wasn't all she was hiding from him tonight. The Camerons spotted someone else they knew and moved to the side, and Marcus stepped up to the stocked bar, debating on whisky, wine, or beer.

"You and Lily of the Valley. I don't envy you, Black," said a voice from behind him.

He turned to find Emmett drinking a beer from a glass,

his eyes focused across the room where Lily had just come inside from the balcony. She locked eyes with Marcus, smiled, and then realized who he was talking to, and her steps faltered.

"She really is sleeping her way through the industry, isn't she?" Emmett said.

"Did I not make myself clear backstage?" Marcus asked, leaning in closer to the asshole running down his girl.

"What are you going to do, punch me out in front of every one of your peers?"

"Maybe."

"Marcus." Lily's soft voice tore his attention away from Emmett, and he found her beside him, looking a little nervous and a whole lot beautiful. He looped an arm around her, but she pulled away slightly. Which pissed him right off.

Emmett raised his beer. "Like I said, I don't envy you. When she's hot, she's hot, but when she's cold—"

Before he thought about doing it, Marcus drew his elbow back and socked Emmett in the face. "No one talks about my girl like that."

He stumbled back, spilling his beer, the glass shattering on the floor. The crowd let loose a collective gasp.

Shit.

He lowered a hand to help the bastard up, but Emmett, with the help of Reginald London, was already struggling to stand.

Shit. Shit. Shit.

"Marcus! What did you do?" Lily was halfway to Emmett, and seeing her on her way to tend to him was enough to make him see red.

"I don't think so, McIntire." He pulled her to him,

gripping her upper arms and tugging her close. "You're with me." Overcome by adrenaline and just plain want, Marcus slammed his lips over hers.

He let her arms go, wrapping his own arm around her lower back and pulling her close, as a different gasp came from the crowd. Lily curled her hands into the lapels of his tuxedo jacket, moaning softly against his lips.

That. Was more fucking like it.

The kiss ended and he heard a whistle or two—probably Clive, the ass—and a few golf claps. Emmett stood off to the side, covered in beer, but not bleeding, just looking like he had swallowed a frog he couldn't quite hack up.

"What the hell!" Lily's two small hands landed squarely in the center of Marcus's chest and shoved.

He felt his head shake side to side.

"You couldn't wait until we left?"

He took in the room full of well-dressed industry leaders, and Emmett's dishevelment, and told her the truth. "No. I couldn't."

She blinked, aghast. "You promised."

"No. I never promised. And if you think I'm going to stand by while that dickhead talks about you like that, you're dead wrong."

"I don't need you to fight my battles for me," she said, her voice wobbling.

That hit him like a fist. No. Like a glove filled with bricks. All he heard was "*I don't need you.*"

"I can't believe you'd do this to me." Her eyes filled with tears.

"I did that *for* you." He leaned closer. "What about what you're doing to me?" he asked between his clenched teeth.

She put one shaking hand to her forehead. "I...I need to get home."

"No. I'll go. Let you do some damage control." He practically spat the words. "One last dare, Lily." She froze, her eyes growing wide. "I'll be at the mansion if you need me. If you don't show, well. I guess you lose."

And so would he. But there was only one way to find out if she was willing to walk away from her ex and face her fears—especially those she had involving him. And that was to go back to the site where his lips had first met hers. Where they were raw and honest and couldn't hide how they felt.

Without looking back, he walked for the exit, passing Clive and earning a pat on the shoulder that said his best friend would back him up even though Marcus had just punched London's new right-hand guy in the jaw.

And then he left—left Lily behind to make her decision. Either she would stay and try to smooth everything over, or she would finally trust him and follow where he was leading.

It was her call.

He was done being the needy one.

• • •

What. Had just. Happened?

Lily pulled her hand from her forehead, blinking at the staff cleaning broken glass and beer from the parquet flooring. Emmett was toweling off his suit and shoes, pausing every so often to glare over at her.

And Marcus was...gone.

She could either follow him and tell him all the things she'd decided on the balcony...or stay here and try to explain herself to London before Emmett started spinning his web of lies.

And what could she say? Marcus had kissed her in front of everyone. And it wasn't a peck. Wasn't a friendly, we're casually dating smooch. It was a *kiss*. A we-burn-the-sheets-up-when-we're-together lip-lock that left no doubt that they were horizontally mamboing with the best of them.

So now to decide if she cared what everyone thought of her...

Did she?

"Ms. McIntire."

She jolted at Reginald London's surly voice over her shoulder. When she turned, she met his craggy face and unsmiling mouth. His stone-gray eyes tracked to Emmett, who scurried to his side.

"Sir," Emmett started, lifting a finger to point to where Marcus just vanished.

"I'll deal with you later, Webster," Reginald grumbled.

Lily jerked her eyes from her ex to the older man, who offered her a smile that actually reached his eyes. "Lily McIntire. Go get your man," he said with a wink.

Emmett's face was a priceless mix of worry and shock punctuated by a reddening welt from Marcus's fist.

Joanie appeared with Clive as Lily took a step away from the forming crowd. "Sorry. I may have pulled Reginald to the side and spilled the beans."

Lily grasped her friend and pulled her into a hug. "I've never been happier that you can't keep a secret."

"You heard London," Joanie said, holding Lily at arm's length. "Go get your man."

She started for the exit then turned back. "I don't have a car!"

Clive slapped his keys into her hand. "We'll get a cab. Do what you need to do."

"Clive…"

"We've got your back, Lil. Always."

With a watery and grateful smile, Lily ran for the parking lot so she could drive to the one place she swore she'd never return.

. . .

She wasn't coming. He knew it.

Fuck, he knew it in his gut. The more he turned over her expression, and the expressions of everyone in that room, Marcus knew there was no way Lily would leave the dinner without doing damage control.

And he'd let his pride ride shotgun and publicly humiliated the woman he loved. And for what? The satisfaction of punching out the dick who had caused her so much pain in the past. It was immature. Childish. Selfish.

Marcus had wanted to claim her, when what he should have done was protect her. He still would have punched the idiot, but he didn't have to grab her up and kiss her in front of the crowd. Seemed like the thing to do at the time, but he'd taken it a step too far.

Damn.

He kicked the deflated air mattress to the side, next to the rest of Lily's goods and wares that he had come to retrieve. Then he headed upstairs, careful of the gaps and cracks in the flooring, and turned left into what was supposedly Essie Mae's former bedroom. Tonight was as dark and spooky as the last night he was here, but he was so damned brokenhearted, he thought all his childhood nightmares—Jason, Freddy, and Pinhead—could have all appeared and Marcus wouldn't even be able to summon up a good set of goose bumps.

He bent and picked up the device he'd stashed in the closet. He pressed a button and a tinny voice said one word.

"Go."

"Yeah, Essie," he said. "I'm going."

He stood, bone-tired and husk-empty, turned... and encountered a beautiful pale-skinned, strawberry-blonde hovering in the doorway, wearing an emerald-green dress.

The sight of Lily nearly stopped his heart. He swore, and then put a palm to his chest. "You scared the shit out of me, McIntire."

She shrugged then gestured to the recorder in his hand. "You're a cheater."

"Kind of."

"That explains the voice," she said, "but not everything else."

Not the footsteps, the crashing sound, the fact that he and Lily had come together that night and several times since.

"No." He shook his head. "Guess not."

A small smile found her face in the dimness of his flashlight's beam, and it was like the sun had come out after a year of darkness. His heart lifted. It had to mean something that she was here.

"I was afraid of more than this place." She took a wary look around the room, as if waiting for something to jump out at them. But whatever activity had ramped up the night they'd first made love was not here. He could only feel Lily, only feel his love for her stretching between them like a strong band.

"I was afraid of trying again," she admitted. "Afraid of being judged. Of people talking about me. I didn't want to give them a chance to shun me. Not again."

"Lily." He took a step toward her, needing to touch her. She held up a hand and arched a prim eyebrow. He stopped in his tracks.

"I dare you, Black."

His lips curved into a smile. "Dare me to what, McIntire?"

"Try," she whispered in the surrounding darkness, "to only kiss me once."

"That's a bet I'll lose." Erasing the space between them, he caught her head in his hands and kissed her long and hard, until she was climbing him, clawing at him, messing up his hair, and making his pants too small in the crotch.

A creak that sounded a lot like a door swinging open echoed from another part of the house. He looked down at Lily in his arms and saw that her lust-filled eyes were quickly sobering.

"Maybe let's do this elsewhere," he suggested.

"Yes. Good idea."

He took her hand, weaving their fingers together, and started down the stairs, carefully maneuvering her around the gaps. "My place or yours?"

"How about Hawaii?"

He paused at the front door. "Yeah?"

She nodded and grinned.

"My place first, though," he said.

"And what about all that?" she pointed back to the discarded air mattress and other paraphernalia.

"We'll get it next time," he promised, and then hustled her out the door.

Epilogue

There were more umbrellas in Lily's piña colada than there were dotting the semi-private beach laid out in front of her. She stood on a blanket of white sand framed by a turquoise ocean and a sea of palm trees blowing in the warm Hawaiian breeze.

She took a deep breath, coconut suntan lotion and fresh ocean air mingling in her senses.

"You're such a tourist," Marcus quipped from her left.

"I'm in Hawaii. I'm drinking what the locals drink." She frowned at the massive fishbowl glass in her palm, already beginning to melt. "Since you're a spoilsport, I brought you a beer." She abandoned her drink on the small table next to her chair and walked over to the hammock where he sprawled, naked save for the jaunty board shorts riding low on his hips. She placed the ice-cold bottle on his abdomen and watched with delight as his abs clenched.

He sucked in a startled breath, clamping onto her arm as

he pulled the bottle away from his body. He didn't let her go, lowering her instead to his waiting mouth. "Vixen."

She smiled. "Asshat."

Their mouths met for a kiss that threatened to buckle her knees. Before she knew what was happening, she was being towed into the hazy, gauzy oasis of lust only he seemed capable of bringing her to. If she didn't put the kibosh on this kiss, she'd haul him back to their cabana for some afternoon delight...*again*.

He pulled away from her first, and a stubborn protestation sounded low in her throat. His toothy grin would have better suited a predator with a pointy dorsal fin.

"Later, toots," he said, hand trickling down her back to cup her bottom. "You've nearly worn me to a nub over the last two days alone."

His fingers slipped beneath her bikini bottoms to touch one cheek. She stepped out of his reach. "Fine," she said. "If you need a break." She walked to her beach chair, knowing he watched her. She shouldn't tease him. She needed a break, too. She ached in muscles she didn't know she had. Sleeping with the sexiest man on the planet would do that to a girl.

He remained quiet, letting her have that last dig, then slid his sunglasses from his nose to his head and closed his eyes. She watched him in the dappled shade of his beachside bed, admiring the sexy way his hair brushed his forehead.

Since the night of the RSD dinner, the same night her ex tried to bully her and Marcus stood up for her honor, they'd grown closer. As often as possible, he made good on not letting her leave his bed. And she made sure she escaped to her own house at least once or twice a week. But just before this trip, she realized her lease was up. And she did not re-sign.

When he saw the paperwork on her kitchen table, and the fact that she'd checked the box that said she was not renewing, Marcus had pulled her against his body and kissed her deeply. It had sort of gone unsaid that when they returned from Hawaii, they would relocate the contents of Lily's house to Marcus's. Sometimes a kiss said so much more than words. And she hadn't tired of learning *and relearning* the physical language between them. At this rate, she'd be fluent in no time.

"Macadamia nut for your thoughts," Marcus said, bringing her back to present.

Lily lounged in her beach chair, an unread novel open against her stomach, her drink more liquid than slush. She blinked over at him. He was leaning across the hammock, arm outstretched, the nut between his thumb and index finger.

When she reached for it, he pulled his hand back. "Ah-ah. You have to tell me what you were thinking about first."

She felt her cheeks heat.

His eyebrows jumped. "Again?" he asked with mock seriousness. "You filthy girl."

The laugh that bubbled out of her only escalated when he rolled from the hammock and yanked her out of the beach chair. The book fell from her lap to the sand, and she stumbled to keep up with him.

His hands landed on her butt, and he squeezed her cheeks in his palms. "Let's go play in the waves," he said, lowering his head and stealing a kiss. "Deep, dark waves where no one can see what my hands are doing."

She reached for the drawstring on his shorts. "Or mine?"

He grinned down at her, his thick hair blowing in the

breeze. "Especially yours."

When his arm banded around her thighs, she squealed. He tossed her over his shoulder and walked her to the shore while she held onto the waistband of his shorts for dear life. He carried her until they were knee-deep in the ocean and put her down, scooping handfuls of cool water onto her sun-soaked skin. She shuddered, her body going stiff against the surge of sudden cold.

"What are y-you doing?" she asked, shivering.

He dropped another handful onto her midriff and chased the rivulets over her bare stomach. "Acclimating you to the temperature."

She smirked. "Copping a feel is more like it."

"Yeah, that, too." He poured water over her shoulder, trailing his hand down her arm slowly. His face grew serious.

She put her hand on his. "You all right?"

"I was just thinking about the mansion," he said, not meeting her eyes. "If you hadn't made that bet…"

They wouldn't be here together now.

"If you hadn't tried to scare me out of the house," she added.

He smiled his wicked smile—her favorite. "If you hadn't thrown yourself at me on the air mattress."

She drew back and splashed him. Marcus squinted, salt-water dripping from his eyebrows and rolling off the tip of his nose.

He grabbed her waist and gave her a long, deep, slow, wet kiss. One she might not recover from any time soon. When they parted, he said, "Okay, that was me. Hard to admit…like other things I can't admit."

The uncharacteristically sheepish glance he cast to the

side made Lily brace for impact.

"If I say it, don't freak out."

Doing her best to appear innocent, she widened her eyes. "I won't."

He quirked his lips. "No…I don't believe you."

"I promise." She couldn't keep the million-watt grin from lighting her face.

"No." He shook his head. "Now it's turned into a thing. I'm not going to say it."

She tugged his neck and kissed him full on the mouth. "Silly boy, you just did."

He frowned. "No I didn't."

"Oh, yes you did. You dropped your gloves, left yourself exposed. Gave away your position." She waded out to deeper water, splashing and singing, "Marcus Black loves me, Marcus Black loves me!"

"I never said that," he called, following after her, his thick legs slashing through the water as he walked.

When he caught her, he scooped her up, holding her thighs as she wrapped her legs around his waist. One of her top five favorite places to be. She put her arms around his neck as the tide sent water sluicing between their bodies.

"What about you?" he asked. "I don't hear you making any heartfelt admissions."

She traced his lips with one finger and avoided looking into his dark eyes—eyes that held more truth than she could handle some days. Not to mention that admissions, heartfelt or otherwise, weren't exactly on her list of things she was good at.

"On three," Marcus said, his voice low.

She lifted her eyes, her heart thudding with a combination

of fear and anticipation. "One, two, three, then go? Or one—"

"I love you, Lily."

"Oh."

He lifted an eyebrow. "Oh?"

"Wait, you caught me off guard. That's not what I meant to say." She clung to his neck like a barnacle as Marcus grasped her butt in his palms. "Don't toss me!" she shrieked. "I'll say it! I'll say it!"

He lowered her against his chest again, buoying her in the deep water. "You've got three seconds."

She blinked up at him. "But that's crazy, right? It's so soon."

He kissed her, and it was no different from any one of his kisses before, but her heart beat extra hard, her blood pumping extra fast.

"I knew you couldn't say it," he said when they parted.

"Can so."

"Bet you can't."

"Bet I can." She tightened her arms around his neck and leaned in, brushing her nose against his.

His wide, genuine smile warmed her heart. She admired his handsome face in the sunshine and swallowed down her fears. With great risk came great reward.

Marking his lips with a soft kiss, she whispered, "I love you, too, Black."

He grinned against her mouth.

"Yeah," he said, leaning his forehead onto hers. "I know."

Acknowledgments

A long, long time ago, in a galaxy far, far away...I wrote a short story for a call for submissions. A little more than a year later, the story sat untouched on my hard drive while my agent continued to sing its praises. The timing wasn't right until just now, and I'm *thrilled* Marcus and Lily get their day in the sun!

Thank you, first and foremost, to God, for gracing me with more blessings than I deserve. It's a bit of heaven on earth, this job. I once read that writing was the act of taking "divine dictation" and I must agree. I am grateful every day for the words that come, even though I'm never *exactly* sure where they're coming from.

Readers, it's thanks to you I put pen to paper (or fingers to keyboard). Because of your willingness to spend time reading my words, I have a reason to write them.

Sincerest thanks to my critique partners for the former and current versions of this book. Michele Shaw, for your eagle eye and accuracy in pointing out errors. To Piper Trace: it is with pride I admit that there are a few lines in this story that belong to you. If I can return the favor, please let me know. Lauren Layne, you answer the tough questions. Shannon Richard, you laugh at my jokes (and thank you for letting me use your Donald Duck one).

To my agent, Nicole Resciniti, thank you for loving this story (and Marcus!). You worked for a year to help this book see the light of day, and your comments and editorial remarks were spot-on. Thank you for telling me the original short story had a great big heart. That compliment went a long, long way, and gave me room to grow it into a full-length novel.

Last but most definitely not least, to Liz Pelletier. When I met you at RT 2013, your comment to me was, "Someday..." I'm proud to say that *someday* is *now* and *If You Dare* is my maiden voyage at Entangled! Thank you from the bottom of my heart for your editorial comments and your pinpoint honesty.

About the Author

A former job-hopper, Jessica Lemmon resides in Ohio with her husband and rescue dog. She holds a degree in graphic design currently gathering dust in an impressive frame. When she's not writing super-sexy heroes, she can be found cooking, drawing, drinking coffee (okay, wine), and eating potato chips. She firmly believes God gifts us with talents for a purpose, and with His help, you can create the life you want.

Jessica is a social media junkie who loves to hear from readers. You can learn more at:

JessicaLemmon.com

Twitter @lemmony